I0589321

IN THE EYES OF MADNESS

By Michael Pang

DEDICATION

I dedicate this book to my wonderful wife who continuously provides me with the encouragement to make this all possible.

ACKNOWLEDGEMENTS

I'd like to thank my brother, Danny Pang, for being my multiple draft guinea pig for almost three years.

PROLOGUE

Zoe and Tristan Sullivan were rudely awakened by the sound of knocking on their bedroom doors. It was three in the morning. The incessant knocking rang loudly inside of Tristan's skull as if someone was banging his head against a wall. Tristan had barely fallen asleep from a night of drinking when the knock came. In anger, he picked up the cell phone on his nightstand and threw it against the door. The phone created a gaping hole in the door. Nervously, the old Sullivan family butler, Vin, poked his head near the hole and spoke, "Young Master Tristan, there is an urgent call from the Orange County Sheriff's Office in Florida. Something has happened to your parents!"

Still annoyed, but pressing down his anger, Tristan combed his hand through his black hair. He answered, "Vin, you've worked for our family, for how long now? You should know better. What could have possibly happened to my parents?"

From down the hall, Tristan heard the yelling of his twin sister, Zoe, as she stomped from her bedroom. "How many times must I tell you losers? Don't wake me up for anything!" A loud crash sounded near Tristan's bed. Apparently, Zoe had ripped a sconce off the wall and thrown it at Vin. Luckily, Vin had dodged the incoming projectile, which penetrated through the door and ended up in Tristan's room.

Stammering, Vin uttered, "Mah ... mah ... Miss Zoe, please forgive me, but it is urgent. It's a phone call from the Florida Police. Your parents were found ... found ..."

Zoe impatiently shouted, "Well, spit it out! What? Are you getting senile? What are you hesitating for? You've already woken up the entire household. Come on now! Stop wasting my time."

Tristan calmed himself as he exited his room and into the hallway. "Come on Vinny, you can do it ..."

Vin shielded himself and prepared for any type of injury the two young masters might inflict on him and said morosely, "Dead. The police believe that they might have found your parents' bodies, and they request that you go down to Orlando to identify them. I am terribly sorry. I cannot believe how this could be possible, but apparently the bodies they found had your parents' identification and belongings on them. And I tried calling them, but received no answer."

The blood drained out of Zoe's face and her demeanor completely changed. The look of anger and menace disappeared as worry consumed her.

"Why are you telling me these lies, Vin?" asked Tristan as he looked at the change in Zoe's demeanor. The anger he was trying to hold back overwhelmed him. "Are you and Zoe playing a trick on me? If you are, know that it's not funny and that I'm not very forgiving," he demanded as he approached the old butler. He grabbed Vin by the arms that were shielding his face.

"Please master Tristan, please don't. I'm just the messenger. That's what the police told me, please don't," cried Vin before he screamed in pain.

Zoe looked up from her phone after a failed attempt of reaching her parents and yelled at Tristan, "Stop it, Trist. Nobody's playing any tricks. Let's just take a trip to Orlando and see what this is about."

This is just not possible. I won't believe it until I see it, he thought.

CHAPTER 1
-DECLAN-

Declan Peters strolled down the halls of the Central Florida Behavioral Center. The hallways, painted a different color depending on which wing he was on, didn't necessarily cheer up the patients. Some were depressed, hanging their heads while they walked around aimlessly, while others, high on their meds, interacted with whichever television show was currently playing, or played board games. He gave a hand wave to a few of the patients that he's come to know, and some of the volunteers who were visiting with them. The center was lucky to have them.

He recalled the most recent volunteer fundraiser and how the director, after a few jokes, became serious and told the crowd what they wanted to hear about: the AIPP program. The director didn't talk long so they wouldn't get antsy but told them about the program. AIPP stood for Adolescent Inpatient Psychiatric Program and was a program for at-risk youths to help them assimilate better with society by providing a nurturing and less restrictive environment. Typically, there wouldn't be volunteers at a behavioral center as identities of the patients were at stake, but AIPP aimed at helping youth function and interact socially. Declan looked upon the volunteers with gratitude as Andy Smith, a local pastor who brought the volunteers to the center every week, walked past him. He was one of those cool and hip pastors who led different youth groups around the city doing community service. He even dressed like a local teenager, with his skinny jeans, Henley shirt, and hoodie. Although his ID card would reveal the fact that he was 59 years old, his demeanor, sharp grey eyes, and smooth skin often misled others to believe that he was at least 20 years younger. As Andy walked past Declan, he snapped his fingers ending with his index finger pointing at Declan, winked, and said, "Good to see you, dude." As part of his weekly ritual, Andy stopped at every door to perform a quick, silent prayer for each of the patients.

Declan cringed. *Why does he have to do that? It should be illegal for old folks to look and act like that.*

He liked the fact that the pastor brought volunteers to spend time with the patients, but the whole religion aspect of it turned him off along with the pastor's attempt to connect with the youth by trying to be one. Declan's aunt and uncle were devout Christians who constantly reminded him of what Christ had done for him and how God loved him. Although they had good intentions, Declan felt their beliefs were being forced upon him, and he tended to get defensive quickly.

Despite how Declan felt about religious volunteer groups coming through the center, he found it soothing to be at work. It might seem strange for someone to find their work environment soothing, but creating a relaxing atmosphere is part of the requirement for any type of behavioral hospital. At the center, the walls were painted neutral honey beige, and there were vases of flowers everywhere. The smell of lilacs filled Declan's senses as he strolled down the hall.

It didn't resemble the movies where all the walls are sterile white, and the rooms are padded with white cushioning, by any means. There were no creepy blue-greenish florescent lightings that would make visitors' skin twitch. The third floor, where Declan worked, was dedicated for AIPP patients. For the sake of the center's image, the third floor was kept pristine and friendly, and nothing like the old mental asylum horror films.

It wasn't just the ambiance the center provided that had given Declan peace. He felt a certain sense of warmth knowing that *she* was near. Declan had spent a good amount of his childhood at the center. He visited his mother who had been committed since he was seven years old. Even throughout his middle and high school years, he spent countless weekends with his mother, caring for her. After many years, the staff at the center knew Declan well. By the time he was seventeen years old, he easily convinced the director of the center to hire him as an Unlicensed Assistive Personnel, or UAP. This allowed him to help his aunt and uncle with the bills.

The center needed people who could easily restrain athletic teenagers who were fueled by hormones and adrenaline. Declan was a perfect fit. He loomed over most of the patients due to his height, and he had a build like an Olympic gymnast.

Declan loved working at the center. He was mainly hired as "the help" to the medical personnel there, but he loved to chat with the patients. He delivered their food or transported them between floors for examinations. Even some of the more unpredictable patients with violent tendencies didn't faze him. He didn't feel that there was any real danger here for him to worry about since the patients known to be dangerous were on the fifth floor. Here, the patients were younger and Declan never hesitated to get more personal with some of them.

Today, however, something was different. As he walked down the hall, a new patient was being admitted. Normally, he would jump at the chance to meet and familiarize himself with a new patient. Creating a comfortable environment for the patient was key to their recovery; however, something inside him resisted this newbie's friendly personality. He felt his feet freeze onto the floor as prickles of ice flowed through his body. Slowly, he looked at the new patient. He looked to be a young man in his late teens, about Declan's age. His ghastly pale skin contrasted fiercely with his pitch-black hair, spikey and messy.

Seeing patients around his age had always given Declan pause. Some say that mental illness is hereditary. If that was true, then he could very well be a patient at the center one day, just like the patient before him.

He took a closer look at the patient's sullen face and noticed the dark circles around his eyes. His body appeared malnourished and frail. Although his body language conveyed that he was relaxed, his eyes showed agony and conflict. As he gazed into the eyes of the patient, the hairs on the back of his neck stood up and goose bumps ran down his arms. It was hard for Declan to grasp the gut feeling that he had about the patient, but something felt terribly wrong.

Nothing strange going on here. We're in a behavioral hospital; some patients are bound to make me uncomfortable, he thought as he tried to reassure himself. *Besides, I'm at least a head taller than him.*

Declan walked up to the admissions counter ready to start some small talk with the patient, but redirected his attention at the last moment and spoke with his coworker, Joe Shum. Joe was about twice Declan's age, with a little bit of grey starting to show on the sides of his head. If it weren't for the graying of his hair, he'd hardly looked a year or two older than Declan. He was about a hair shy of being six feet tall and had a herculean physique.

Seeing Joe sparked a memory of their last camping trip and how the tent almost caught fire. They laughed about that for months. He was sure glad Joe took him under his wing since he didn't have any siblings. Declan loved to think of Joe as his big brother.

Joe had been an UAP at the center since Declan's first visit ten years ago. At the time in his life when Declan had thought that he had lost everyone, Joe had been there for him. Throughout the years, they had formed a strong bond. Outside of work, Joe had taken Declan bowling, camping, and to watch all kinds of sporting events when Declan was in middle and high school. In a way, Joe also was a father figure to Declan as his own father had passed away before he was even born. When Declan met Joe, he couldn't help but to latch onto him emotionally.

Throughout his childhood, Declan had asked his mother about his father and all she would say is that he had passed away. She would then get teary-eyed and too upset to say more. When the other kids' dads picked them up from school, he would look upon them with envy. At night when he flipped through his mother's old photo album, he would imagine what his life would have been like if his father was still around. They would play catch in the backyard or maybe he would teach him how to shoot hoops. Bedtime would be filled with adventurous tales by both his parents. But then, the day came when his mother was admitted to the behavioral center and he lost her too. He then moved in with his aunt and uncle, but the topic of his father was taboo in their house because it made his aunt too upset to talk about her dead brother.

Maybe Joe's presence helped him overcome that gut feeling he was having about this patient. "Hey Joe, how's it going there? Care to introduce me to our newest guest?"

Joe turned toward Declan as he approached. "Hey Declan, we're doing just great," stressing the word "great" the way that Tony the Tiger used to do in the television commercials. After years of working with young patients, Joe had incorporated many different cartoon character impressions into his speech. Unfortunately, after his divorce three years ago, he decided to consume himself with work as a distraction. He got so used to doing the impressions that he was no longer capable of stopping himself even when he was speaking with older patients and coworkers.

Joe continued. "This is Kyle, we're just getting his paperwork done while his parents finish his registration downstairs. I thought that I'd help Kyle get a head start so that his parents can help him get settled into the room when they are done."

"Hi, Kyle. My name's Declan, and I'm here to help out. Please let me know what you need, and I'll try to make your stay here as comfortable as possible. Feel free to call for me whenever you need; even if you just need to talk," said Declan, while keeping the last part in a whisper. Officially, Declan and Joe were just UAPs, but they pretty much took it upon themselves to also be "friends" to the patients on their floor.

Kyle stared at Declan. Although there were no facial movements, Kyle's eyes were moving wildly. Not with very noticeable movements, but rather subtle, yet rapid shifts in every direction. Declan couldn't shake the feeling that Kyle was crying out for help, but for some reason, he wasn't able to get the words out or think to try out any other bodily movements than his eyes. Those eyes seemed to scream for help, but when they coincided with the body language that conveyed tranquility, it made it difficult for Declan to decipher what this patient was really trying to say. Declan had always prided himself on his ability to read how a person was feeling, and the contradictory eyes and body of this patient really disturbed him.

"Yes, Kyle. Declan is a good boy," Joe said patting Declan on the head, sobering Declan out of his thoughts. "He will take very good care of you while you're here. I've known Declan since he was a little boy," he added, making a hand gesture suggesting that Declan was about waist high back then. He continued, "And there's no one here with a heart bigger than his. So, you're in good hands." Declan gave Joe a quick glare. He always got annoyed when Joe treated him like a kid, and Joe knowingly continued the practice.

Why does he keep doing that? How am I going to get any respect around here if he keeps doing that in front of everyone? Declan fumed.

Kyle remained motionless and continued to stare. Rosy, who worked at the admissions desk, broke the silence. "Alright sweetie pie, your paperwork is all done and you're gonna be in room 305," she said in her usual southern drawl. A sweet but vengeful woman of 53, Rosy was like a mom to the workers at the center. Rosy's desk was littered with photos of her children and grandchildren. In addition, a curious picture of a beautiful teenaged girl with long silky blonde hair and perfect skin stood at the corner of her desk. The photo was an obvious vanity glamor shot taken at an expensive photo studio. Compared with the sweet lady with giant crow's feet and white hair, the way Rosy looked like today, no one would have ever guessed they were the same person. The regulars knew the real truth because every now and then Rosy likes to brag.

"Sweet as she is, that gal did not age well," Joe said on many occasions while Rosy was away from her desk. Once, Rosy overheard Joe, and she made him pay for it over the next couple months. Whenever there was a "messy" job that needed to be done, Rosy would call Joe to do the cleanup. "Like all southern gals, sweet, but aren't to be messed with," Joe concluded at the end of one of Rosy's retributions.

"Declan, would you like to come with me to show Kyle his room? I'm sure he would love the company," asked Joe as he turned to Declan and gave him a pleading expression. Declan realized that Joe also felt something strange about Kyle and wanted him to join them.

"It would be my pleasure," replied Declan as he secretly patted Joe on the back letting him know that he understood his concern.

As they walked Kyle to his room, Declan still couldn't fight the feeling that something was wrong. His palms started sweating profusely, and a trickle of sweat rolled down his forehead. A chill went through his body as ice prickled the back of his neck.

As they walked down the hall, Declan reviewed the list of amenities that the center offered with Kyle. The stroll toward Kyle's room felt endless as Declan tried to fight down the feeling of alarm that was screaming inside of him. Declan continued to run through the center's scheduled meal times and visiting hours. He kept talking the entire time, not only to inform Kyle but also as a means of distracting himself from the distress he was feeling from within. As they got to Kyle's room, Declan proceeded to open the door just as Andy Smith came out of the room next door.

"Hey, Andy. Let me introduce to you our new patient. His name is Kyle. Kyle, this is Andy. He's a local pastor who brings a group of volunteers to the center. He and his group of volunteers come by every week to talk to the kids. They put on fun events every so often too." Joe and the pastor showed off a special handshake that included fist bumps.

Declan raised an eyebrow as he watched the old guys trying to act like young guys.

"Great meeting you, dude. I hope that you find your stay here a blast. The peeps here are great, and with God's grace they will get you better ASAP," said Andy with a big warm smile. Although Declan was once again turned off by the mention of God, he couldn't help but feel some of his distress alleviated by Andy's presence.

"I want to go to my room now," said Kyle who turned abruptly toward his room.

Declan and Joe were startled from Kyle's response. "I think Kyle is tired, Andy; we're going to go get him settled in," Declan quickly responded. Andy wasn't Declan's favorite in terms of volunteer coordinators, however, he was offended when people were rude to the pastor. Since Declan was a kid he'd known Andy, and he could testify to how the volunteers had helped the patients recover. Whether it was truly the grace of God or not, Declan could not deny the patients' progress.

"Well, I'll be seeing you later, dude. Hope you get up to snuff soon," said Andy, as he turned and said a quick prayer for the room he was about to leave. Declan and Joe were walking into Kyle's room to get him settled as Andy placed his hand on Kyle's door. His next stop was Kyle's room, and he started saying a silent prayer for Kyle.

Just then, Kyle violently turned toward the pastor and yelled, "Leave me alone!" The voice that came from Kyle sounded so foreign and so utterly wrong that it sent shivers down Declan's spine.

Kyle ran toward the pastor, and Joe caught him by the arm to try to stop him. With inexplicable strength, Kyle took hold of Joe and threw him at Andy by using one arm. Joe collided with Andy and fell. Declan instinctively jumped onto Kyle's back, snaking his hands underneath Kyle's arms to restrain him, before he could do any more harm to Joe and Andy. As his hand made contact with Kyle's skin, he felt an overwhelming gloom that seemed to destroy all that was sunny and happy. All the feelings of dread and misery that Declan had ever felt in his life surged out from all the repressed corners of his mind. He felt that he would prefer to be dead rather than to live the rest of his life. As the sense of coldness spread across Declan's body, he felt almost frozen.

Kyle started to spin to try to throw Declan off, and it jogged Declan out of his gloom. He tried to use his weight to pin Kyle down, but Kyle was much stronger than he appeared. He stood as if there was a mere child on his back. Kyle started spinning faster, but Declan held on tight.

"Help, guys, help! What are you waiting for?" shouted Declan as he clenched his legs tighter around Kyle's abdomen. He kept his eyes closed because he felt that if he opened them, he'd be sick all over the linoleum floor from all the spinning Kyle was doing.

Joe ran into the room with a sedative shot he'd pulled out of the locked medical cabinet outside the room. He leaped onto both Declan and Kyle to add the extra weight to help pin Kyle down, but immediately, he was flung off, and he fell hitting his shin on the bed table. "Ahhh!" he screamed.

Declan managed a shout to Joe. "Throw it to me!"

Joe carefully tossed the sedative to Declan. It arched toward the ceiling and Declan held one firm grip on Kyle's arm while he held up his other hand. He caught the shot and grabbed it tightly. "Got it!"

He looked at the tranquilizer in amazement, almost proud that he had caught it despite the chaos and shouting. But his conquest was short-lived; Declan hesitated a fraction of a second too long. Using his newly freed hand, Kyle grabbed Declan off his back and with a loud grunt placed Declan into a tight chokehold in front of him. Declan started to make gagging noises and his eyes widened with terror when he realized that Kyle's free hand was inching toward his neck. He struggled but Kyle was too strong. When the injection went into his neck, he screamed.

Immediately, darkness crept into Declan's vision and threatened to overwhelm him as deoxygenated blood flowed through his brain. Luckily, the sedative worked quickly.

Just before Declan lost consciousness, Kyle's arms fell limp and collapsed, letting go of Declan. He crumpled to the floor, gasping for air.

Bright colors now substituted the darkness and filled his eyes as oxygen flowed through his veins and back into his brain.

Rosy ran into the room with Kyle's parents. They couldn't believe what they saw. It looked like a battlefield. One man was on the ground, dazed, almost loopy, one was in the corner, grimacing from pain, and the other was sitting in a corner with his head in his hands, breathing heavily.

Rosy noticed the used syringe on the floor in front of Kyle. "Oh dear, what happened? We heard a lot of yelling from down the hall. Are you boys okay?"

Joe slowly got up from the floor, limped over to Declan and helped him up to the bed. He tried to explain as much as he could remember, with everything happening so fast.

They all turned when they heard footsteps running in the hall. Finally, several large nurses' assistants came in to take Kyle away. When the nurses' assistants visited, you knew you were in trouble. They were two of the biggest and strongest men on the payroll, and they were hired for these instances.

After Kyle left with the nurses' assistants on either side of him, each holding one arm, it was quiet in the room. Kyle's parents stared dejectedly down at the floor, not knowing what to do. They never saw their son in such a rage before. They were frightened and held onto each other for support.

Rosy touched Kyle's mother gently on her shoulder. "I'm sorry." Kyle's mother could only nod.

"Let's get you back to the office and we can talk, okay?" Rosy led Kyle's parents out of the room.

Declan, who was still feeling the effects of the asphyxiation, felt sorry for Kyle's parents. He heard them openly sobbing as they walked down the hallway towards Rosy's office and his heart shattered into a million pieces. He felt his eyes burn as tears flowed from them; the incident was all too familiar to him. He saw himself as a little boy once again, sobbing loudly as the policemen dragged his mother away. He shook his head to try to clear it.

Joe called his name, and it broke him out of his thoughts. He turned and saw that Joe was sitting down, still recovering from the whole ordeal. Joe, rubbing the bumps and bruises he received from the incident, muttered in his best Garfield impression, "I hate Mondays." Declan gave Joe a small smile.

Suddenly serious, Joe complained, "I can't believe how strong that kid is. Did you see how he was able to pick me up single-handedly? I've never seen a patient with anorexia have that much strength left in them. As a matter of fact, I've never seen anybody, patient or not, with that much strength in them. How in the world were you able to restrain his arms for so long, kid? You don't even have a scratch on you." Joe added in his Bugs Bunny voice, "I know this defies the laws of *physics*, but I never studied law!"

Declan smiled again shaking his head. "Adrenaline, maybe? I don't know. Besides I was behind him most of the time, so it wasn't like he could strike me or anything. And what do you mean without a scratch? My neck still hurts from being strangled."

Joe teased, "Aw...did Declan get a booboo? Come here; let me take a look at that booboo." Joe laughed but winced as he clutched his ribs. "You know, you're pretty lucky. With that kid's strength, he could have easily broken your neck."

"What do you think set him off anyway? I've never seen any of our anorexic or autistic patients have violent episodes like that. He seemed especially hostile toward Andy," said Declan pensively.

"Maybe he was one of *them* "altar boys" when he was younger. Or maybe he just didn't like his room. Who knows what sets our patients off? It sucks when it happens, though, especially when they've been here for a while and you've watched them progress. From my years of experience here, there isn't always a rhyme or reason as to why they do the things they do." Joe gazed off into the distance the way he always did when he was serious.

"I don't know, Joe, he just seemed like he wanted our help. I don't know why, but that's just my gut feeling."

"You'll get used to it after a while. You've only been working here for about six months; it isn't uncommon for some of our patients to have a meltdown. You're gonna want to help each and every one of them, but don't forget that's the doctor's job. Our job is to keep them from harming themselves or harming other patients while they're here. Don't think about it too much. Wanna go grab a bite? Our shift is almost over."

Joe stood up and walked toward the elevation. Joe, realizing that Declan hadn't followed him, turned back and added in his Shaggy impression while dropping his serious gaze, "Let's do what we do best, eat!"

"Sorry, Joe. I have dinner plans tonight. I'll see you tomorrow though. I'm going to stop by my mom's room before I leave," said Declan as he walked past him and pushed the "up" button for the elevator.

As Declan walked toward his mom's room on the fourth floor, he couldn't help but think of Kyle's parents' faces as they saw their son lying on the floor unconscious.

Once again, he saw himself as a kid when the police had to come to take his mother away. His mother was always so warm, kind, and gentle. He remembered the feeling of her warm hands on his cheeks. The warmth would spread from his cheeks all the way down to his heart. He remembered her long, straight black hair tickling his face as she bent down to kiss his forehead while she tucked him into bed. Most of all, he remembered those big brown reassuring eyes that made him feel that everything was going to be alright. She had never even raised her voice at him. He knew that he had felt nothing but love coming from her as a child.

But then one day, she just…snapped.

The image of the police restraining his mother as she tried to pull toward him resonated through his mind. She had just tried to drown him in the local community pool. Luckily, the lifeguard there had noticed her and stopped her in time.

"You don't understand! It's the only way! I won't let you have him! Leave my son! If you hurt him, I swear I'll kill you," screamed his mother with the look of menace on her face.

Snapping himself out of his memories, Declan approached his mother's room, clutching the pendant that hung around his neck. The pendant didn't have any expensive embedded jewels, just a smooth stone with a few symbols carved on it. It was one of the few articles of jewelry that Declan had found amongst his mother's belongings soon after she was committed. Ever since he was seven, he wore that pendant around his neck. And whenever he thought about his mother, he would unconsciously clutch at the pendant as if trying to grasp and hold on to a time when everything had been good.

His arrival at his mother's door broke him out of his thoughts, and he realized that he was clutching his pendant so hard that the symbols had imprinted onto his palm. He stared at the door for a few seconds as if deciding whether or not he should turn around and leave instead. He took a deep breath. When he placed his hand on the cold doorknob, goose bumps traveled up his arm. He was hesitant to open the door because he didn't know what state of mind she would be in. Taking in another deep breath, he swung the door open.

Declan's mother greeted him with a smile. She looked healthy; rosy cheeks, fair skin, and big warm brown eyes. The same eyes that had always given Declan peace. "There's my boy. How was your day honey?"

Declan let out the breath he had been holding since he stepped over the threshold into her room. My day was fine, Mom. How are you feeling today?"

She walked over to him and gave him a long hug. "I feel great!"

Declan felt tears threatening to well up in his eyes as his mother embraced him. From the day that he just had, he was afraid of what state of mind he might find his mother in. "Do you need anything? Can I get you some more water or blankets? I hear that it might get a little cooler tonight." Declan quickly turned to the thermostat and adjusted it so that his mother wouldn't notice that he had teared up.

"No worries, I'll be fine." Mother took a breath and had a shine to her brown eyes like she was excited. "I had a chat with Dr. Lanier today...

"Oh really, mom? What about?" Declan didn't know what to expect and was a little nervous about her announcement.

"He said that I might be able to come home with you soon. I can't wait to get out of here!" She clapped her hands she was so excited. "It's been too long!"

Declan nodded encouragingly. He had heard this before but she never came home. It was just her wish, and he already knew the outcome.

She smiled tentatively. She figured out that Declan wasn't really interested and suddenly changed topics. She leaned forward, wanting to please. "But enough about me, you told me yesterday that Caleb came into town last night. How is he doing?"

Caleb and Declan had been best friends since the second grade. They used to do everything together, but when they graduated, Caleb went off to college, while Declan had to start working to help support his aunt and uncle.

"He seemed to be having the time of his life last time I spoke with him on the phone. I'm supposed to have dinner with him tonight. I guess I'll hear all about his awesome college adventures then. Yay..." he replied sarcastically as he walked over to the window and looked out at the setting sun.

At least, Keira will be there, he thought as his face started to heat up.

"As soon as I'm out of here, Declan, I promise you I'll help financially, and you can go to college," she said, interrupting Declan's thoughts. "I know that it's been hard for you and your uncle and aunt. As a matter of fact, I've been working on a little something. I made these during craft time. I think I can sell them as jewelry and maybe make a business out of it. Here let me show you." She walked toward a box on her nightstand and took out a flower with a string on it. It was an orchid that had been preserved in some sort of glossy resin. The sunlight from the setting sun reflected brightly on the glossy flower, making it shine radiantly.

"That's beautiful, Mom. I bet you there will be people who would want to buy these." Declan examined the flower while taking hold of his mother's hands. He felt his hands burn and looked up when he thought he saw something move in the corner of his eye. Suddenly still, his mother was staring off into the box. As calmly as he could manage, he asked, "Mom? What are you looking for? Mom?" He got no response from her, and he felt a chill go down his spine. The remainder of the setting sunlight seemed to have withdrawn from the room. A sense of panic engulfed all his senses, and suddenly she looked up, grabbing his arms.

He shuddered as she suddenly screamed out. "You can stop pretending to be my son! I will never tell you!" She grabbed Declan by the back of his shirt collar and dragged him toward the bathroom. Struggling to free himself from his mother, he thrashed his arms and legs around trying to grab hold of something.

Choking, Declan managed to shout, "Stop, Mom! Please stop it! I'm your son! Can't you remember? I'm your son! Please, Mom, don't do this!"

She bashed Declan's head against the base of the bathroom sink as she tried to push Declan's head into the toilet bowl. Pain exploded from the side of his head, and everything started to look blurry.

"I will drown you this time, demon child! You took everything from me! I won't let you hurt anyone else!"

Declan pushed off with his arms and legs and slammed her against the bathroom wall opposite from the toilet. The room seemed immensely longer than it had been as he ran back to her bed to push the call button for one of her nurses.

He had almost reached the button when she grabbed him by the hair to drag him back to the bathroom. "Not this time! I've got you this time!" she screamed.

Declan reached out once again toward the hospital bed where the call button was located. The bed moved forward a couple of inches and Declan's finger collided with the button. Despite having to fight off his mother, he squeezed his eyes shut for a second when he thought he must have somehow hallucinated the hospital bed's movement.

Hospital beds don't move by themselves! He wondered if this was all real.

Within twenty seconds, three UAPs rushed in and restrained his mother. She continued to struggle and hiss, screaming, "I will get you, demon! I will kill you if it's the last thing I do!"

Declan walked out of the room. His eyes burned as tears streamed down his cheeks. He said, "Goodnight Mom, sleep tight," as the doors closed behind him.

CHAPTER 2
-DECLAN-

It had been three years since Declan's mom had a violent episode, but it always seemed to come back. Tonight was such an example.

Just when it seemed that she was normal. Just when everything seemed to be okay, she would revert back to that day. What happened to her on that day that made her snap? How could someone so gentle and sweet all of a sudden become so violent? Why would she want to harm me? She loves me. I know she does. Did I do something wrong? What could I have possibly done wrong? I was just a child...

Mental disorder is hereditary. Does that mean I might snap someday? Will I try to kill someone I love? Who will I hurt? Whose life will I destroy if they see me lose it?

Such thoughts haunted Declan's mind as he drove back to his home in Winter Garden clutching onto his pendant as if his life depended on it. Whenever Declan felt down, there was always one thing that would cheer him up...gelato. He felt as if the coolness from the Italian ice cream could freeze his pain, and he could then lock it up in a repressed corner of his mind.

Moreover, before his mother was taken away from him, she had always brought him to get gelato in the afternoons. Whenever he did anything that deserved a reward, gelato was the reward. So now, the gelato shop, Anthony's Gelato, in Downtown Winter Garden, had become his happy place.

Declan parked his car at the lot on Lakeview Avenue and walked toward Plant Street to Anthony's Gelato. As he walked, he felt the familiar brick walkway under his feet, and it brought back the feeling of happiness that he had experienced before his mother was committed. The cool breeze coming off of Lake Apopka channeled between the large brick buildings and flowed against his face and through his hair. He felt as if it had taken away some of his sorrows. One of the reasons he enjoyed living in Winter Garden was the fact that while the rest of Central Florida was covered with stagnant humid air, Winter Garden always had a cool breeze running through it due to its proximity to the largest natural lakes in the area. Another reason was the people. As people walked by, they greeted him with warm genuine smiles, and Declan knew that he was home in this town.

The gelato shop looked almost like it had the day that his mother snapped. Anthony didn't feel that his shop needed any updates or anything. The poster taped to the window for as long as he could remember, read, "Try our new flavors!" The featured flavor had apparently been considered the new flavor for the past ten years. The diner-style booths and tables also never went out of style because every couple of years it would come back and be considered "retro." Sure, it wasn't the coolest or hippest place to be, but their gelato was unbeatable. Although Declan didn't really know Anthony personally, anyone who could make such delectable nirvana was okay by Declan and deserved his money.

He purchased three scoops of chocolate hazelnut gelato in a cone and sat at a table next to the window. He could remember the day that he lost his mother so well; it was as if it was yesterday.

Declan had gotten a hundred percent on his spelling test, so his mother was treating him to gelato.

"Mommy, mommy, can I have two scoops of chocolate hazelnut gelato?" asked Declan as he jumped up and down with glee.

"Are you sure you can eat two whole scoops of gelato? You might get a tummy ache."

"Oh please mommy. I can handle it. I'm a big boy now," replied Declan with a big smile on his face and a strong man pose with flexed biceps.

"Well of course you can, my smart boy. Why don't you get us a seat by the window, and I'll get our gelato." She smiled warmly down at him with pride in her eyes.

"Okay, mommy." Declan skipped over to the table by the window. Knowing that his mom enjoyed watching people stroll down the street, he sat with his back to the window so that his mother could have the seat facing the window. It was a quaint little town, and the people were honest and kind. It had that small town feel where almost everyone knew their neighbors and were always willing to help each other out. The residents voted to preserve the historic look of the town, but nothing looked run-down or dirty because town pride was very important to the residents and they kept everything pristine.

"Here you go. For a job well done," she said proudly as she handed Declan his cone with two scoops of gelato. She placed her hands on his cheeks. "But you know I would have bought you gelato even if you didn't do as well on your spelling test, right? You are the most precious gift in my life. And I love you more than anything in the world."

Declan had always loved that warm feeling from his mom's hands as she cupped his cheeks. "I know, Mommy, and I love you too. Can we go to the pool later? I want to practice my swimming so that I can beat Caleb next week at the YMCA."

"Sure honey, but we need to wait at least a half an hour after gelato, otherwise you'll get sick." She was looking out of the window when her smile suddenly faded. Crease lines formed around her eyes as they turned hard. From the bulge in her jawline, Declan could tell that her teeth were clenched. Declan hadn't seen such a look on his mom's face before. "Actually, Declan, why don't we get a head start walking over to the pool? By the time we get there, I think it should be fine for you to swim then. Do you still have your swim pants with you in your book bag?"

"Of course, Mommy, I'm always prepared to go swimming," Declan said as excitement spread across his face, and as he quickly disregarded his mother's sudden look of worry.

"Come on, Declan, let's get going." She quickly gathered up their things.

Declan's flashback ended when his gelato dripped onto his shirt. He looked at his watch and realized the time, as he tried to wipe off the gelato. He finished eating his gelato as he hurried back to his car.

CHAPTER 3
-TRISTAN & ZOE-

Tristan and Zoe walked into the Orange County morgue. Zoe's skin crawled and goose bumps ran down her arms. She felt cold all over and her bones started to shake.

"Follow me, Mr. and Ms. Sullivan," said the deputy on site.

The coroner, Robert Halls, approached them quickly upon their entrance. He was a short and stout fellow, with greasy brown hair. Tristan cringed as he gazed upon the appearance of the stocky man.

How does one working with dead bodies all day have the appetite to eat enough to become so rotund?

Robert, looking shaken, spoke directly to the deputy escorting the two teens. "Deputy Johnston, I don't know how to explain this. The bodies, they've...deteriorated at an alarming rate." Suddenly, as if only just realizing the Sullivans were also there, he jumped ever so slightly. "Mr. and Ms. Sullivan, I'm very sorry, but I'm afraid you don't want to see this. I will do a computer analysis of the bone structure to reconstruct the facial features. Although, I have to say, that the features on the corpses when they first came in was a match to the photos on the IDs for David and Lydia Sullivan. But it is the procedure for the identification to be done by their kin. It will only take a couple of hours."

Tristan paled, but at the same time, a flare of anger appeared in his eyes. "Did you say that the bodies deteriorated? How long would you estimate that they've been dead?" He demanded of the coroner in a somewhat shaky voice.

Robert blinked at the question. "Well, when the bodies first arrived, I estimated the time of death to be within the past sixteen hours."

"No I mean, by looking at the corpses right now, how long ago would you estimate the time of death to be?"

Zoe looked confused by her brother's questions and then seemed to come to a realization. The blood in her veins became ice cold, and she felt queasy as her hands shook violently. Looking as if she was going to vomit, she forced out with whatever breath was left in her, "Tristan, stop it. I don't want to know. Please don't ask anymore. I don't want to hear this." She quickly turned and ran out of the morgue.

Ignoring his sister, Tristan pushed again. "Well...how long?"

"I don't see the relevance. I am definite from my experience that they died within the last sixteen hours." Robert held up his hands in defense. "I can't explain how the bodies have deteriorated like they did..."

Anger exploded inside of Tristan and his vision became red as he grabbed the coroner by the collar. "Based on how they look now, how long ago was the time of death?" he shouted.

Deputy Johnston, being the big and tall man that he was, had always been able to demand authority. He placed a calm hand on Tristan's shoulder. "Son, calm down. I know you're upset right now, but calm down and let Robert run his analysis. We can confirm the identities of the bodies with the results."

Tristan considered killing the deputy and forcing the answers he wanted out of the coroner as his fist balled up tightly, but decided against it. He relaxed his hands and dropped them to his sides. "I'm sorry, but can you please just tell me what would be the new estimated time of death based on the current deterioration?"

Robert, indignant, fixed his collar abruptly. "Like I said, I don't see the relevance, but if you have to know I'd say at least 15 to 20 years."

Tristan's shoulders slumped, and he walked out of the morgue. As the doors closed behind him, his knees went weak, and he fell to the ground. His fist clenched and eyes burned, but sounds of sobbing pulled him from his anger. He looked up and saw that the sounds came from Zoe.

He looked around and realized that he was kneeling on the floor. Standing up and dusting off his knees, he trudged over to his sister. When Zoe looked up to see Tristan, she said: "Don't tell me; I don't want to know."

Tristan replied with a blank look on his face. "They lied to us."

"No, I won't believe it. We still haven't confirmed if those bodies are Mom and Dad yet." Zoe's voice was full of hope. "Maybe Mom and Dad were pursuing them and somehow they dropped their wallets near the bodies when they killed them."

"Then why haven't we heard from them? Why haven't they been answering their phones? Let's face it, Zoe. What do we know about bodies that deteriorate like that? Remember Georgia?" pushed Tristan.

Zoe turned away from Tristan as her eyes seemed to glaze over. She took a deep shaky breath, and the flashback of what had happened two summers ago in Georgia flooded Zoe's mind. It was the first time that the Sullivans had taken the twins "hunting."

"Zoe! Get him into the water," yelled Zoe's mother, Lydia. Zoe grabbed the 46-year-old archaeologist, the same man they had pursued for the past five days, and they plunged into the lake together. He struggled against Zoe for a few seconds before his overwhelming speed and strength were gone. Zoe, who had a hard time catching up to him for the past couple of days, now zoomed past him. Ten minutes earlier he had overpowered her and threw her like a ragdoll, but now she was able to easily restrain him.

"Not so fast anymore are you? So that's your little secret," said Zoe as she punched him in the face a couple of times. "Tell me demon, what have you extracted from this host so far?" she demanded.

Holding his nose, which appeared to be broken, the archaeologist stammered, "That's impossible. How are you unaffected by the water?"

"That's because I'm the real thing, you loser! Not some halfwit—"

"Zoe! Don't reveal more than you have to." Zoe was cut off by her mother.

"The real thing…impossible, we were wiped out. Unless you're a…" The archaeologist broke out in cynical laughter. He then looked at Lydia and sneered. "You know that's forbidden. I'm going to have you brought in and your daughter destroyed."

"We don't want to hear your lies. You're no longer able to exert anymore magic onto this host, now as the remnants of your touch washes away from the body, it will start to revert," Lydia said with a cold smile.

He looked at his hands and saw that she was telling the truth. His hands started to thin out and became wrinkled. His entire body shook. Tilting back his head to open up his airway, his mouth opened wide and a writhing shadow started to climb out of it.

"Don't let him escape! Fully submerge him," Lydia shouted.

Hesitantly, Zoe pushed his head under the water, and his hands started to flap and struggle. As the archaeologist continued to writhe, tears streamed down Zoe's face as she looked at her mother with a plea. Zoe's heart pounded inside her chest as a minute passed, and the struggling archaeologist's movements slowed.

Am I really going to kill him? She thought.

Within two minutes, his hands stopped. When the body floated to the surface, it was completely…skeletal. Zoe screamed.

CHAPTER 4
-DECLAN-

Declan was so deep in thought that he didn't even notice Uncle Roy approach him as he parked and exited his car. Roy was what people would consider an all-round average man. He was about five-feet-eight inches and had a build that was neither skinny, muscular, nor rotund. He had a full head of white hair and sharp blue eyes. Although Roy looked average to most, to Declan, he was the epitome of a real man. He always welcomed everyone with open arms, always kept his word no matter the consequences, and always spoke out for what was right.

"Hey Deck, I thought you were having dinner with the Millers tonight," Roy said as he pulled Declan in for a hug. Declan pulled away but couldn't help but smile when he saw the smudges of grease across his uncle's forehead.

"I am. I'm just parking my car at home and walking over. I didn't want to crowd up the street. You're home kind of early. How was your day, Uncle?" he asked.

"Oh, I've had better days. Unfortunately, I was sent home early today. My hours are going to be cut to two days a week. There's just not enough work at the foundry in this economy. I don't know what we would do if you weren't working. Did I tell you how much we appreciate you helping with the bills?"

"That's the least that I could do, Uncle. You guys took me in and raised me as your own when my mom was…taken away. Think of it as my repayment for burdening you guys all these years," replied Declan as he hesitated to talk about his mother.

His uncle's smile subsided. "Declan, you're the best thing that has happened to your aunt and me. We've tried to have children for years, but that was just not part of God's will for us. And then, He blessed us with you. You were never a burden to us. Don't ever think that way. You owe us nothing." Roy's eyes watered up.

"I know, I know. You've said this many times… Well, I like working at the center anyway. So, it's fine," said Declan as he tried to reassure his uncle, probably for the hundredth time.

"It's only going to be a short period of time. The owner of the foundry is going to install a new furnace tomorrow. It's supposed to be top of the line. He hopes that this will open us up to the super alloy market. He's putting the last of the company's money on this gamble. But I think it's a sound decision. If our business does go back up, we'll be fine, and you can go to college. Maybe Valencia or something." Uncle Roy's voice was hopeful.

Valencia was a local community college that many of Declan's school friends were currently attending. It was considered to be a good stepping-stone into getting into one of the better state Universities. Declan's aunt and uncle were not wealthy and even while still in high school, Declan knew that Valencia was about all they were ever going to be able to afford. However, when Declan graduated high school, the economy crashed and even Valencia was out of the picture.

"College … I don't know, Uncle. Can we really afford college? I mean, who wants to spend four years in some classroom while accumulating a mountain of debt? I could be making money at the center during these four years instead," declared Declan trying to sound uninterested.

"Son, life isn't just about the money. Going to college will get you out of your comfort zone. Meet new people. Find new opportunities.

Don't waste your talents. You had excellent grades in high school, held offices in multiple school clubs, won so many awards at state level fairs, and you're intelligent. You deserve to venture out," replied Roy, sounding proud as ever.

"Alright, alright … when that time comes, I'll think about it. Where's Auntie?" asked Declan trying to change the subject.

He didn't want to get his hopes up about going to college, only to have them crushed again. Declan was certain that he would have been able to get a scholarship to go to any college he wanted with his good grades and the extracurricular activities he was involved in. However, he was not awarded any of the major scholarships that would have allowed him to attend. When he questioned the different committees that granted the scholarships, he was told that there was a policy in place that put a quota on the number of scholarships that were awarded based on ethnicity to show that there was no discrimination in the selection process. Unfortunately for Declan, his Asian heritage seemed to have put him at a slight disadvantage.

"It's Wednesday, so she's probably at the soup kitchen. She'll be back soon."

"Maybe you should take advantage of the situation and take Auntie on a 'date night.'" said Declan, using finger quotes and grinning.

"Now that you've mentioned it, maybe I will take your suggestion to take my gal on a date night. Don't come home too early if you catch my drift…" Roy grinned.

Declan made a face. "Gross!"

Roy noticed the gelato stain on Declan's shirt and his grin faded. "Hey buddy, what happened today?"

"What do you mean what happened?" asked Declan as he put on an innocent look to hide his pain.

Roy frowned when he saw Declan's expression completely change. "Something must have happened today…I see the gelato stain on your shirt."

"I don't want to get into it right now, Uncle." Declan glanced down to the gelato stain.

"You know you can talk to me about anything Declan. You're like a son to me. Don't shut me out now."

"Mom had another violent episode today," Declan said suddenly, trying to hold himself together.

Roy's face paled a little bit. He walked over to Declan and gave him another hug. "Are you okay? Were you injured?"

Declan couldn't hold it in any longer and his words came pouring out. "Injured, no. Am I okay? How can it ever be okay? My mother is crazy and tries to kill me every so often. How is any of this okay?"

"My boy, everything happens for a reason. We may not understand why it has to happen this way, but God has a plan. We might not see the bigger picture, but your Heavenly Father does. I just know it, Deck, God will make something amazing out of it."

Anger surged within Declan. Throughout his life, everyone who had known about his situation had given him the same consoling words: "God has a plan." Ever since he lived with his aunt and uncle, they had reminded him that everything happens for a reason and only according to God's plan. The more he thought of his life and the more people said those words to him, the more he hated hearing them.

Declan pushed his uncle away as his face glowed red with anger. "God has a plan? God has a *plan*? Oh, that's great! The all-loving God has a *plan* that involves my mother who is normal one second and an attempted murderer the next. If that's God's plan then I don't want to have anything to do with Him."

He wanted to tell his uncle how much he hated his life. How much he hated God's plan. And to a certain extent, how much he hated his uncle and aunt for constantly forcing their beliefs on him. He knew that he needed to get out of there before he said anything else he'd regret.

Declan couldn't say all those things to his uncle. He was angry, but he wasn't cruel. He realized how much his uncle loved him. So he decided to simply walk away. "I'm sorry, Uncle. I have to go. I'm running late."

A tear came from the corner of Roy's eye as he watched Declan disappear down the street. "Heavenly Father, please lift Declan up and soothe his heart. I don't know why his life has to be so hard. I know that you have a plan, and I should be patient. But God, it's breaking my heart to watch this happen to him."

Roy's prayer broke into a sob. That didn't deter him though. He continued to plead. "Please Father, have mercy on us. Let us in on your grand design. Through the good and the bad, we will praise you, because we know that you work for the good of those who belong to you. Father, please hear our cries and soothe our hearts. In Jesus' precious, holy name I pray, Amen."

CHAPTER 5
-DECLAN-

Declan walked toward the Millers' house, five blocks down from his. He was glad that he had the five blocks to clear his mind and pull himself together. Feeling bad about the way his conversation with his uncle had ended, he decided to have another talk with him later that night to apologize. He cleared his mind as he passed houses on both sides, and he felt his anger subside.

Seeing the houses in his neighborhood always had a calming effect on him because they reminded him of the times before his mother was committed. They had a certain character to them. The citrus boom during the forties and fifties had made Winter Garden one of the largest orange providers in the world. In fact, most of the houses in the area were built during that time. Despite the downturn in the local economy during the past couple of decades, the residents still put their best efforts into preserving their heritage.

The Millers' house loomed like a mountain in the midst of low valleys, as it was the only two-story house on the entire street. Declan ran his fingers through his hair to attempt to tame it and straightened his shirt to make sure that he was presentable. Irritation crept up as he saw the stain on it again.

I should have changed my shirt, he thought just as the door opened. *Dang it! If Uncle Roy hadn't distracted me!*

Keira jumped out to her porch to give Declan a big hug. "Hi Deck, how are you? I missed you!"

Declan's cheeks flushed crimson red as Keira continued to hold him in an embrace. Standing before him was the most perfect girl that he had ever known. Her skin was like a porcelain doll and her silky blonde hair flowed across her shoulders like beams of sunlight. Most striking of all her features were her mesmerizingly bright blue eyes, which made Declan smile from within. Although she had a petite build, she was quite the athlete and captain of the girls' high school soccer team.

He hadn't seen her since graduation, five months prior. She seemed to have grown even more beautiful while they were apart. He loved her ever since they met in the second grade. Although they were the same age, he was a grade ahead of Keira because he had skipped the first grade through testing.

He recalled when they had first met. He will never forget it. As he sat on the tire swing sobbing, the week after his mother was committed, Keira walked up to him and asked, "What's wrong?"

Keira always had a heart of gold in the sense that she genuinely cared for those around her. She was very observant and seemed to almost have a sixth sense for detecting how someone felt, regardless of how well they hid it. Moreover, she had an aura about her that made people pour their hearts out to her and feel better after doing so.

"Nothing! Leave me alone! I just want to be alone! Go away!" exclaimed Declan as he wiped the tears from his eyes.

"Are you sure? Mommy says that talking about things always makes you feel better. Don't you want to feel better?" Keira ignored Declan's plea to leave as she sat down on the swing next to his.

Declan really wasn't in the mood to talk, but the aura around Keira and her genuine concern was irresistible.

"My mommy...they took her and won't let me see her," Declan replied as more tears welled up. Somehow saying it out loud had made it feel more real to him. In the corner of his mind, he still held the hope that it was all one big nightmare that he would wake up from.

Keira seemed curious. "Who took your mommy, and why won't they let you see her?"

Declan hesitated, not wanting to think about it. But her questions brought him back to the moment when his mom's face suddenly changed from a warm smile to a look of anger and even hatred. He was swimming in the pool, showing off how quickly he could swim. As he came out of the water, he saw the transformation of his mother's demeanor and expression as she watched him from the side of the pool.

"You! You did this to me! You've taken everything from me. I won't let you do this to me anymore! Die..." she screamed.

Declan didn't hear the rest of what she was screaming, since she had placed her hand on his head and dunked him underneath the water. Things started to go black. When he opened his eyes, he was lying on the pool deck with the lifeguard, while police officers restrained his mother.

She was still screaming. "You don't understand! It's the only way! Don't let him out of the water!" Declan had never seen that look on his mother's face before. The grimace that was on her face was as if everything about him disgusted her. She clenched her fists so hard that all the veins on her forearms bulged. Thinking about it sent shivers down his spine and the hairs on the back of his neck rose.

"Is your Mommy sick? I wasn't allowed into my mommy's room either when she caught the flu," said Keira, her voice jolting seven-year-old Declan out of the disturbing swimming pool episode.

"Yes, she is sick," replied Declan, not wanting to say any more about his mother.

"You'll get to see your mommy soon. My mommy got better from the flu after a couple of days. Then she was there to tell me my bedtime stories and tuck me in at night again," said Keira, trying to reassure Declan.

"I hope so, because I have to stay with my Uncle Roy and Auntie Jenny right now. I really miss my mommy. I wake up in the middle of the night, and I get so scared. She usually comes to my room when that happens. But now, she can't come to my room anymore." Declan allowed the dam of tears that had been building up to since he watched his mom being shoved into the police car to trickle down his face. He didn't understand why he would say all those things in front of a girl, but the words and tears kept pouring out.

"Don't be scared. You know, you're never alone. There's someone who will always be with you and will love you no matter what." Keira placed one of Declan's hands between hers. Up until that point, girls had been infested with coodies, but when she held his hand, Declan felt that it might be okay to be contaminated. As a matter of fact, it felt nice.

Of course, she was talking about Jesus and not herself.

Declan blushed a little more thinking about the day that they met and nearly jumped when Keira waved her fingers in front of his eyes.

"Hello...Deck? You're doing that zoning out thing again! Well, come on in. What are you waiting for? I made so much food for you guys." Keira gleefully shook her head as she normally did whenever she had to pull him back from his daydreams.

The old Miller home was warm and cozy. Neutral tones flowed throughout the house along the tan walls, fluffy brown carpet, and rustic wooden furniture. The Millers were practical people. They didn't have a lot of tacky décor like some people, but their walls were covered with family photos and Bible verses.

The large living spaces felt welcoming and people loved to gather there. Every time Declan walked through the Miller's home, he was filled with awe. There was nothing glamorous or expensive that he noticed, but a tremendous feeling of love and family often overwhelmed him. He didn't feel any lack of love from his aunt and uncle, but there was just something different about the Millers.

Caleb walked down the stairs when he heard that Declan was there. He approached Declan while holding out his hand.

Keira and Caleb had apparently won the genetic lottery from their parents who looked like life-sized Ken and Barbie dolls even after their kids had become teenagers; however, Keira was small and petite while and Caleb was tall and athletic.

That jerk, he doesn't even workout, Declan thought to himself. Declan had always been supportive of Caleb throughout their middle and high school years. They were as close as brothers, to the point where they even shared clothes. Caleb went through a phase where he was embarrassed about the clothes his parents bought him. However, when Caleb left for college and Declan was left behind, resentment started to build within him. He even felt jealous of Caleb.

The two clasped their hands together, pulled their chests together, and clapped each other on the back. "Deck, how's it going? So glad you came. Dude, I have so many stories to tell you," said Caleb excitedly, a little too self-absorbed to even allow Declan to answer him.

"Glad you're back, too. Can't wait to hear them," replied Declan sarcastically. Caleb apparently missed the sarcasm and started talking about a sorority girl he met a month ago.

As she watched her brother talk about himself like he always did, Keira noticed the stain on Declan's shirt and immediately knew something must have gone terribly wrong. She wanted to run up to Declan and hold him in her arms, but it would have created an awkward scene with her brother standing right there.

"Hey Deck, did something happen today?" asked Keira interrupting Caleb's story.

Declan instinctively took his right hand and clapped it over the gelato stain on his shirt. "What happened? Nothing happened."

The two Millers looked concerned. They had seen Declan's gelato binge a couple times in their lives. Almost every time, it occurred after a relapse in his mother's condition.

"Let's sit and talk." Caleb led Declan to the dining room where there was a gourmet meal waiting for them. They were having roast duck, corn bread, fresh garden mixed greens and fruit salad, collard greens, mashed potatoes, grits, and yams.

Amazed at the spread of food on the table, Declan took in the aroma. "Wow Keira, this looks amazing! Did you make all of this? When did you learn how to cook?"

"Oh, I took cooking classes over the summer. It wasn't that difficult." Keira blushed slightly.

"How long did it take you? This is a lot of food." Declan was still in awe as he took in another whiff of the aroma and his mouth began to water.

"Most of the afternoon but nothing is too good for my big bro and best friend. It's my pleasure. Besides, I wanted to practice for Christmas dinner next week."

"Yeah…right…it was for me, huh? I came home last night, and you made me a peanut butter and jelly sandwich!" Caleb joked with a smirk on his face.

Keira elbowed Caleb in the ribcage. "That's because you got in at 2:00 am, and I wasn't even sure if you were going to eat."

Declan realized that he was smiling the widest smile. No matter what had gone on that day or how long it had been since they'd seen each other, these two had always been able to bring a sense of happiness within Declan that he couldn't explain. Seeing the two interact always made Declan wish that he had a sibling.

Keira clapped her hands. "Let's eat and talk; the food is getting cold. What do you guys wanna drink?"

"Water, please," replied Declan as Keira walked into the kitchen.

"I'll have a beer," responded Caleb stopping Keira in her tracks.

"Yeah, nice try. Just because mom and dad are out, it doesn't mean that I will put up with your shenanigans; no under-aged drinking under this roof." Keira sounded way too much like her mom.

A grin spread across Declan's face as he watched the siblings interact. Keira, the most caring and sweetest person he had ever known, had a kryptonite, and it was her brother. Whenever they were together, it was like oil and water. Keira could have infinite grace for anyone who had wronged her, but if Caleb ever stepped a pinky toe of out of line, she was ready to rip him to shreds.

The elder Millers were very involved in church and the community. They were always busy with planning and putting on community events, attending leadership conferences, and church meetings. Keira, who inherited the caretaker gene from her mom, felt that it was her job to keep the house clean and everyone in line while her parents were gone. And of course, Caleb, being the older brother, couldn't stand to allow his little sister to boss him around.

"Hey, I'm your older brother. You listen to what I say and show your elders some respect," demanded Caleb as he puffed out his chest and tilted his head upwards.

"I double dog dare you to take one sip of alcohol in this house. If you do, I'm telling," threatened Keira sounding like a ten-year-old.

Caleb smiled. "I missed you, Sis; sometimes you are like the bane of my existence, but what would I do without you?"

Once again, it made Declan grin. Declan remembered the first time he witnessed their constant bickering. Declan had only known the two for about a month, and they were heading toward the vending machine in the school cafeteria.

"Hey! Don't spend all our money on candy! What about lunch?" asked Keira as she tugged on her brother's sleeve.

"I wouldn't feed what they served here to our dog! What's your problem with candy?" Caleb said as he flung his hand free from his sister and inserted the rest of their lunch money into the vending machine.

"But mommy says that candy is bad for your teeth!"

"Mom also says that TV is bad for you! I don't see you complaining when your stupid *Little Pony* show is on!"

"But I'm hungry! I want some veggies and chocolate milk!" cried Keira as she longingly looked towards the line where the other kids received their hot lunches.

"You're such a freak! Who prefers veggies over candy?"

"I hope you get cavities and lose all your teeth!"

And the bickering never stopped. "I really missed the both of you," declared Declan as he walked up to the two of them and forced them into a group hug.

"You do realize that I haven't moved ... " said Keira, the smile on her face fading as she pulled away from the group hug. "I still only live five blocks from you. You could have dropped by or called in the past couple months. You even stopped coming to church."

"I'm sorry, Keira. I just figured you had SATs, college applications, sports, clubs, and youth ministry and thought you wouldn't have time for me," replied Declan sounding guilty.

"Hey, just chill out a little, Sis. Deck has a full-time job. Besides, what would he be doing with his best friend's baby sister anyway?" Caleb said, wrapping his arm around her to give her a noogie on the head.

"First of all, Caleb, I'm only one year younger than you. So, stop calling me baby sister. And Deck, I'll never be too busy for you. I've known you since I was in the first grade. You're family to me. I know that Caleb is your best friend, but I met you first!" Keira pulled away from Caleb, slapping his hands as he attempted another noogie.

Keira's face turned bright red as she realized that she was putting all her feelings out into the open. She walked into the kitchen to get the drinks.

Awkwardly trying to change the subject, Declan asked, "So ... where are your parents anyway?"

"They're at another one of those leadership conferences ... Summit, Catalyst or something," Caleb quickly replied trying to make things less awkward.

When Keira came back from the kitchen, she seemed to be once again her usual cheerful self. "So ... Declan, would you like to share your day with us?"

"Oh, you know, just a typical day at work. Nothing to talk about." Caleb jabbed, "Oh yeah? Why did you have to go to your gelato happy place?"

"I don't really want to get into it. Let's not ruin the night." Declan tried to change the subject. "So how about you? Tell us about college life!"

"Dude, it's so awesome! It's so nice to be out of the house, and I get to do whatever I want. I have a part-time job, so I can make my own money and buy whatever it is that I want." Caleb cheered up. He loved to talk about his favorite subject: himself.

Declan smirked as he watched Caleb take the bait. To make sure that the subject change stuck, he asked a question. "I thought that your parents gave you an allowance. Couldn't you have just bought whatever you wanted with your allowance? What's the big deal?"

Caleb responded defiantly. "You know how it is. Our family is well off, but we live like we're poor. I'm surprised my parents don't insist that we eat at the soup kitchen. Every allowance I get, my parents have a say in how it's to be spent. Ten percent tithed, thirty percent for donations, thirty percent for lunch, and thirty percent to save up for a car. There's no such thing as having a little spending money. I remember every birthday or Christmas, kids around me would get the most awesome toys or new clothes, but we'd have to buy secondhand stuff. It was embarrassing!"

Keira cut in. "I don't understand what you're complaining about. We had an excellent childhood. I don't need things to be happy. Mom and Dad loved us, and we played all the time. And, I don't see what is wrong with the stuff that we have. Sure it's not new, but it works and the clothes fit. You were like one of the most popular guys in school. No one even noticed your secondhand clothes."

"That's because I look good in anything I wear. And I hide it well," said Caleb with a smirk, sounding proud.

Both Keira and Declan rolled their eyes.

"I think we're much more fortunate than other people. And it's not like Mom and Dad horde their money; they're using it to help others less fortunate.

"Then why don't they help me because I feel less fortunate. Well, I'm tired of living for other people; why can't I just live for me for a while? If I am willing to work hard for it, why can't I have nice stuff for a change? I just can't live like Mom and Dad do anymore," declared Caleb angrily.

"Because living just for yourself is too small! Don't you want to be part of a bigger reality, the reality of God? Jesus teaches us to love our neighbors as ourselves." Keira sounded perturbed.

"If living for God means living like a hobo, then I'll just stay out of God's way. And I would appreciate it if He would show me the same courtesy. Keira, just because Mom and Dad are obsessed with all of that religious stuff doesn't mean you have to be, too! Don't be a Christian just because Mom and Dad are. Think for yourself!" Caleb demanded.

"I do think for myself. Yes, Mom and Dad raised us to be Christians, but I never felt that I was forced. I believe in Jesus because I choose to believe and because of all the things that He has done for me. You know that I pray for you and Deck every day. I pray that you guys can come into a relationship with Jesus. You just don't see the wonders and adventures to be enjoyed when someone has faith in Christ and wants a role in His plans." Keira looked upon Caleb and Declan with hopeful eyes.

"Here we go again, Prayer Warrior Princess Keira to the rescue," declared Caleb mocking Keira.

Declan jumped in. "Guys, can we not argue about religion? It gets nowhere; its either you believe or you don't. Let's just leave it at that." Trying to change the subject once again, Declan asked Caleb a question. "Other than being able to live outside of the house, what's so cool about college anyway?"

Taking the bait again, Caleb continued. "Well, I pledged a fraternity this past semester. I got to meet a lot of cool people; partied a lot and hooked up with a few girls. Those sorority girls were so hot! I wouldn't even want to come back at all if it weren't for you guys. Did I mention that the girls are hot and willing?" Caleb raised his eyebrows a couple of times as he ended that comment.

"Ew, gross, you're going to catch an STD ... Nice to see that Mom and Dad's money is going to good use," Keira replied in a disapproving manner.

"Hey, get off my case, I have a 4.0 GPA. I deserve to party. I thought you were a Christian. Why would you jinx me about catching an STD? That seems mean-spirited," Caleb said mockingly as he crossed his arms.

The bantering from the two Miller siblings continued for another hour before Keira refocused the conversation. "Is something wrong, Deck? You seem quiet?"

"Oh nothing, the food is too good. I'm just enjoying my meal." Declan looked down onto his plate and started stabbing his fork into another slice of duck.

Keira pushed on, "Come on, Deck, I know you better than that. What's going on?"

Keira once again proved that she could get anyone to pour out their sorrows. Hesitantly, Declan gave in and told the two about the ordeal with his mother.

"Dude, I'm so sorry. That is just messed up," Caleb said trying to empathize with Declan.

"Yeah, tell me about it. I don't know how much more of this I can take. One moment she's normal and the next ..." Declan tried to get the words out, but couldn't. He felt a dam of tears building up in his eyes but he looked up to the ceiling so that none could come out.

Trying to help, Keira asked, "Is there anything we can do for you, Deck?"

"You can help me get my mind off of things ... forget even," replied Declan doubtfully.

Caleb grinned smugly. "Thought you'd never ask; just leave that to me. We're gonna party like there's no tomorrow. Get a couple of drinks into you, and you won't remember a thing."

When Caleb noticed Keira's scowl, he grinned and said, "All in the name of helping Deck, of course."

"But I'm not dressed for clubbing," Declan declared, looking down at his gelato stained shirt.

"Don't worry. This time, I'll lend you a shirt."

CHAPTER 6
-TRISTAN AND ZOE-

Robert entered his office where Tristan and Zoe had been waiting. It looked rather warm and cozy for an office located inside of a morgue. There was a light tan couch and a short red coffee table. The desk had a sanded finish that resembled something from the Amish country, and his chair was covered by a fluffy white throw.

Boring office for a boring fat man, thought Tristan.

"So the results are in. Please take a look at the facial reconstruction on the computer screen, and let me know if you can identify the victims." Robert turned his computer monitor toward the two Sullivan teens.

Solemnly, Tristan nodded his head. "Yes, that's them. They are our parents," Tristan said as his eyes watered up. Although his brain had already accepted that reality hours earlier, his heart still held the hope that the two victims were not his parents.

Zoe started crying. "Mom, Dad, what will I do without you?"

Tristan wrapped an arm around her.

"I'll give you guys a moment," said Robert as he walked out of the room.

"I can't believe that they're gone. We'll never see them again!" Zoe cried.

A flare of anger flashed in Tristan's eyes. "Good! They lied to us."

Zoe felt defiant. "You don't know that. Maybe that's what happens when one of us dies. How would you know?"

"Well, why don't we just ask them? Either way, they should be around, seeing that they aren't trapped in their bodies since their remains aren't submerged," Tristan declared. "So why don't you show yourselves!" Tristan jumped up from his chair and paced the room, shouting. "Mom! Dad! Where are you? I know what you are now! Show yourselves!" Tristan demanded, looking around the room, expecting his parents to appear.

Nothing happened. Zoe's lips quivered. "If Mom and Dad are...then what are we? Are we also...?"

"Demons? You can't even bring yourself to say it, can you? No, we are not demons. Water doesn't wash away our powers. I don't know what we are. Are we even their kids? Can they have kids? I don't even know. Maybe they took us from our real parents. Maybe they're not even our parents," declared Tristan angrily.

"Stop it, Tristan. They raised us. They loved us. They're our parents, biological or not." More tears fell freely down Zoe's cheeks.

"Why did they lie to us? They told us that our family bloodline was the last of the Nephilim. That was obviously a lie, seeing that they are demons," Tristan said angrily with the feeling of betrayal fueling his rage.

"Stop it, you don't know that," Zoe pleaded. "I can't stay here. I need to get some air; get a drink."

Zoe left the room, leaving Tristan alone. Tristan thought about the time when his parents first told him about their family bloodline at the age of seven. He was in the backyard with his mother that day after he was sent home from school for fighting. "I had just barely pushed him, Mom, I promise. I don't know how he got a broken rib. Besides, he was a bully and was hitting another kid first," pleaded Tristan tentatively, afraid of the punishment that he would receive.

"Tristan, I know that you didn't mean to hurt him, but you have to be very careful when you are around other kids. You're different from the other kids. You are stronger, faster, and soon you'll also be able to do other things that children your age can't even imagine doing." Lydia held Tristan in a serious gaze.

"What do you mean I'm different, Mom? I don't look different from my classmates. Are we aliens or something?" questioned Tristan with an intrigued smile on his face. Tristan had always felt like an outsider when he was in school because his family had always kept to themselves. He was never allowed to go to birthday parties or sleepovers. Because the other students never got to spend any time with Tristan outside of school, he wasn't able to form any true bonds with anyone. At a young age, he imagined that he was Superman, sent to earth to protect humanity; the earthlings weren't allowed to get too close to him so that they wouldn't discover his secret identity. When his mother mentioned that he was different, he was actually thrilled, not sad.

"Well, I guess you're old enough know our little family secret. We're not the same as the people around us. We may look like them and talk like them, but we are very different. And no, we're not aliens. You see, we are descendants of the angels, and the last of our kind." Lydia had a warm smile on her face, which Tristan misconstrued.

As much as Tristan wanted to believe, it seemed farfetched. With a look of disbelief, he asked, "So we're angels?"

"Not exactly, we're half human. That is why we look no different from those around us," replied Lydia with a cringe on her face as she said the word "human."

Lydia could tell that Tristan was still having doubts. "You're joking, right?"

"Nope, this is no laughing matter, Tristan. Soon, your powers will grow, and you'll have to learn to control them; otherwise, you could end up hurting a lot of your classmates." Lydia showed a strange smirk on her face as if she found the thought slightly amusing.

Tristan was confused. "If we're angels, what are we doing here? Why haven't we met other angels? Can we fly?"

"Half-angel. And I know you have many questions. There are some things that you are just too young to understand. So for now, that is all you need to know." Lydia tried to stonewall the incoming flood of questions by hold up her hand.

"But I still don't believe it. How can we be angels? I don't even fly," demanded Tristan flapping his hands in an effort to will himself to fly.

"Let me show you what you'll eventually be able to do," replied Lydia as she moved so quickly she became a blur.

Amazed, Tristan yelled "Whoa, Mom! That was so cool! Will I be able to do that one day?"

"That and much more," explained Lydia as she picked up a rock and crushed it in her hand. Tristan jumped up and down with glee as he clapped his hands.

Tristan pushed on, "Ooh ooh, one more question, Mom. Why are we just half-angel?"

"Remember the conversation we had last month about the birds and the bees…?" replied Lydia as she hoped not to revisit the awkward conversation.

A knock on the door ended Tristan's reveries. The door opened, and Robert walked in with a stack of papers for him to sign.

CHAPTER 7
-DECLAN-

"Two shots of Vodka," Caleb yelled to the bartender over the blasting music at the local club, Matrix. The club was dark with the exception of the bright flashing strobe light in the middle of the dance floor. The strobe light made everyone look like they were teleporting as they moved about, appearing one second and disappearing the next.

The bartender nodded at Caleb and pulled out two shot glasses for the liquor.

"You know, I'm going to tell Mom and Dad that you have a fake ID. You are in so much trouble, buddy," declared Keira with a disgusted look on her face, shouting into Caleb's ear.

Caleb scowled at Keira and yelled back, "Alright, miss goody-two-shoe. Go off and tell on me to mommy and daddy, whenever you see them. But in the meantime, stop being a buzz-kill … literally. Don't you want to help Declan take his mind off things?"

"You know, getting slugged in the head with a bat will kill just as many brain cells and will force Declan to focus on other things for free," Keira chided as she mimicked swinging a bat with her arms to make it more apparent what she was talking about; it was so loud in the club.

Caleb rolled his eyes at Keira. He handed the bartender money and gave a shot to Declan. "Bottoms up!" Caleb yelled as he raised the shot glass to his mouth.

Declan hesitantly took the shot as he watched Caleb down his in one gulp. He felt the burn of the liquor all the way down his throat and into his stomach. Declan cringed.

"That was so smooth," declared Caleb with an excited gleeful look in his eyes.

Declan cringed, "Are you kidding me? I feel like everything inside me is on fire!"

"Oh yeah! Burns so good," Caleb declared with a big grin.

With that, Caleb talked Declan into taking several more shots with him. After downing three shots, Declan felt a little dizzy. He'd never had hard liquor before.

Keira shook her head and yelled into Caleb's ear mockingly, "I can see why I thought you were dumber since you've gone to college." She then grabbed Declan's hands and said, "Are you just going to drink or are you going to dance?" dragging Declan onto the dance floor.

It was like a dream come true to Declan. He was dancing so close to Keira that he could smell her perfume. Declan was in such bliss that all he had on his mind was Keira. He took notice of every little movement her body made as they danced; it felt as if she had a gravitational field of her own that was drawing him in.

"Deck? Is something wrong? You've stopped dancing," Keira shouted with a smirk. Keira was all too familiar with that look on Declan's face, as it had happened too often. She realized that as she got older, the more effort she put into her looks, the more of that type of reaction she received from him and other boys. Declan didn't realize that he had stopped and was staring at her.

"Oh, I'm sorry, it's just that you look so beautiful today," he said as he blushed.

Keira blushed also, and moved in close so that she could talk to him without yelling, and teased, "Just today?"

"Oh no, you've always been beautiful, I mean…sorry, it's the alcohol talking," stammered Declan and he blushed even more as he felt her body against his.

She continued to jab at him. "You mean you only find me beautiful when you have alcohol in your system?"

Keira was trying so hard not to laugh as Declan continued to stammer while backing up a step. "No, no, no, no, no, no, no, that's not what I meant. I've … I've always found you beautiful Keira. I just never had the courage to tell you."

She reclaimed the step that Declan took. With her lips almost pressing up against his ear she said "Oh, you've always found me beautiful? So…are you going to make a move or something?"

Declan turned to look deep into Keira's eyes. "Something like that." Although they were in a club with music thumping, the smell of beer and sweat, and people dancing all around them, he felt as if they were the only ones there. For him, the only thing that mattered at that moment was her. *Should I move in for a kiss*, he wondered as his heart pounded. *Is she giving me the signal that it is okay to move in?*

But the moment was over all too soon as reality came crashing in, literally; a nearby dancer bumped into him. He fell forward toward Keira, crashing his forehead against her lips.

Keira clutched at her mouth. "Ouch, I think I bit my lip. I think I might need some ice."

Keira and Declan quickly left the dance floor, embarrassed. When they walked closer to the bar, they saw Caleb sitting next to a tall girl.

Declan was going to approach the bartender for the ice, but Keira stopped him. "I think I feel better now," said Keira as she continued to observe Caleb and the girl.

The girl was beautiful with her silky long black hair and long lashes with flawless tanned skin. She was of a long and slender, but athletic, build. She had big round eyes that sparkled, although reddened. Most people weren't pretty criers, but this girl looked beautiful even though her eyes looked like she had been crying for hours.

Keira couldn't resist the urge any longer and walked up to Caleb and the girl. "Hi, how are you? I'm Caleb's sister, Keira. And you are?"

"Hey guys, this is Zoe," Caleb said as he handed Zoe another shot.

Zoe didn't say anything but took the shot. Declan studied Zoe and noticed that she was swaying back and forth in her seat as if she was moving to the music, but she was completely offbeat.

Keira must have noticed the same thing. "Is there something we can help you with? You seem …"

Zoe looked up at Keira and tried to say something. Keira thought that Zoe was obviously drunk by her slurred words. "Yooou waaanna help? Mooore vodkaaa."

Caleb attempted to hand Zoe another shot as Keira intercepted the shot and punched Caleb in the arm. "Stop giving her more alcohol. She's already drunk!"

"What? I'm just trying to help," exclaimed Caleb raising both hands up in surrender.

Zoe gazed at Keira, who seemed a little unfocused, and slurred her words. "Yeeaaah, whhhyy dooooo yooou caaare? Moooore Vodkaaa!"

"Alright, you're coming with me. I don't want anyone here taking advantage of you," Keira said as she glared at Caleb.

"What? I wasn't trying anything. She just looked so sad, and I wanted to help her," declared Caleb with an innocent look on his face.

"And it doesn't hurt that she's hot? Come on, we're going," said Keira as she walked over to Zoe to help her up.

Zoe was still stammering as a guy in a dress shirt, slacks, and suspenders came up to the group. He had one of those faces that women have trouble saying no to; square-jawed, chiseled cheek bones and long, dark eyelashes. He had long, brown, wavy hair that reached his shoulders and made him look like some sort of artist. His frame was rather average, and while he didn't look intimidating to Declan, Declan felt a sense of uneasiness as he approached. He stood between the girls, facing Keira. "I think she said that she wanted to stay and have a few more drinks."

Keira was surprised at how swift he was. "Um ... do you know her?"

"Oh, I know her, and I plan on knowing her a little better," he said with a smirk on his face as he reached out to draw Zoe into his arms.

"Whoooo aaare yoooou? I dooon't knoooow yoooou," stammered Zoe as her head whirled.

"She says she doesn't know you, so she's leaving with us. Creep!" Keira glared at him and pulled Zoe away.

"Do you know who you're talking to? I'm Owen, and I want you all to get out of my club! NOW!"

Owen waved his hands and a few bouncers walked over. These guys looked like they could have been competitors on the American Gladiators' team. They would have been more intimidating, however, if they weren't so round in the midsection. They looked like two giant walking babies.

"No need for escorts. I already said that we were leaving," Caleb said loudly as Keira put Zoe's arm around her shoulders to heave her up with Declan's help.

"I said, leave the girl," Owen demanded as the bouncers walked in front of the group to block them off.

Keira took out her cell phone. "We will walk out of here with this girl or else I'll call the cops."

Owen moved quickly and grabbed the phone out of Keira's hands. Caleb and Declan were shocked at how quickly he moved. "Okay, pal, we don't want any trouble. We just want to leave here with our friend," Caleb pleaded as his hands started to search the counter behind him for anything he could use as a weapon.

Keira screamed at Owen as she tried to reach for her phone. "Give that back!" Others around them noticed the commotion and moved away.

Owen caught her hand and tried to kiss it. "What a bold young girl; I like it."

Declan pushed Owen aside in a rage. "Stay away from her."

"Well, Charlie, are you going to get the first punch or am I?"

"No, Buck, I'll do the honors."

The bouncers moved in, and Charlie punched Declan in the face. Seeing Declan getting slugged, Caleb jumped atop Charlie and broke a beer bottle on top of his head. Buck picked Caleb off of Charlie's back and twisted Caleb's arm, holding him onto the floor. Charlie then went toward the two girls. Recovered from the punch, Declan rushed Charlie, knocking him backward onto a table and crushing it. Buck banged Caleb's head on the floor and went after Declan. Declan was caught off guard as Buck rushed him from the side, put him in a bear hug, and head-butted him.

Thinking that a possible gang-related fight had broken out, all the clubbers started to leave. Girls screamed and people pushed toward the exit.

Both Declan and Caleb were on the floor trying to stop their heads from spinning. Owen walked up to Declan and Caleb and kicked each of them. He then turned toward the two girls. "You guys have cost me some business. How do you want to make it up to me?"

Keira was never so scared in her life, and she backed Zoe and herself into a corner while saying a silent prayer under her breath.

"Stay away from them," Declan yelled as he slowly got up off the floor, holding his side where Owen had kicked him.

Charlie and Buck walked up behind Declan, restrained his arms, and kicked him behind the knees to make him fall back down onto the floor. Owen continued to walk closer to Keira and Zoe, reaching out to Zoe. Keira raised her arm to slap Owen, but he caught her hand. "You know, you only make me more excited when you fight back. No one likes to play with a dead fish." Owen seemed to purr as he pulled Keira in towards him and took a whiff of her hair.

"I said, stay away from her!" yelled Declan. A surge of energy flowed through his body, and he overpowered Charlie and Buck who both tried to hold him down. After recovering from being thrown off balance, Buck tried to punch him. Declan found that it was very easy for him to dodge the incoming punch as it seemed to play out in his mind in slow motion. He then punched Buck in the stomach and down he went. Charlie saw his buddy go down and tried once again to put Declan in a hold, but found the younger man stronger than him. Declan flipped Charlie over his shoulder and pounded him onto the floor.

Owen turned to look at Declan. "Interesting, you can still get up," he said, amazed. He then rushed at Declan at an inhuman speed. To Owen's surprise, not only did Declan see him coming but he held out his hands to stop the incoming blow. Just before the two collided, the lights in the club went out. The place where Owen had expected to collide with Declan was now just empty space.

80C3

Caleb and Keira ran through the back alley between Matrix and the adjacent club with Zoe slumped between them and Declan right behind them. They were running so hard that Keira thought her lungs were about to explode. Declan kept looking over his shoulder to make sure that no one was on their trail. Finally, they were out of the alleyway and into the street where people who had exited the club earlier were now hanging around. The four slowed but didn't stop heading toward the direction of their car before they caught their breath.

"Declan, can you please help carry Zoe? I'm about to pass out," declared Keira breathing hard. Declan was so focused on running and making sure that they weren't followed that he didn't realize that it was Keira and Caleb who had been carrying Zoe the entire time. He quickly fell into place to relieve Keira. She continued to hyperventilate. "Much better."

"Great going, Caleb," said Keira sarcastically, "let's all go to a sleazy club and potentially get raped."

Declan remained quiet. He was deep in thought about all that had just happened. *How was I able to do that? Did I really do that? Did I just imagine it all?*

"Hey, how was I supposed to know that would happen? You were the one who mouthed off to the club owner. Besides, I was the one who got us out of there." Caleb indignantly slapped Declan on the back. "Tell her, Deck! If it weren't for me, we'd all be in a lot of trouble thanks to her big mouth!"

Snapped out of his thoughts by Caleb's slap on the back, he asked, "How did you do that anyway? I was about to get into a fight with the owner. He was rushing at me, I dodged, then everything was dark. I ran toward Keira and Zoe and found that you were already dragging the girls out. So, I followed you guys out and jammed the door shut behind us."

"Well, while the bouncers were busy trying to pound your face in for not staying down, I pretended to be knocked out from the beginning. From all the banter between the creepy club owner and Keira, and your fight with the bouncers, nobody even paid attention to me. I cut the lights for our escape. I thought that we wouldn't be able to fight those two goons, but I guess I was wrong. Where did you learn all those Jackie Chan moves anyway? You took on two bouncers twice your size and won," Caleb said in awe.

So it was all real. I didn't imagine that. Wait, or did I just imagine this whole conversation, Declan wondered.

"Hello! Deck! Focus man!" yelled Caleb.

"I don't know; maybe it's from working at the center. You never know what some of the patients will do and how strong they might be," responded Declan unsure himself. "But, anyway, good move on cutting the lights!"

They finally reached Caleb's car and quickly got in. Caleb started the car and immediately drove off.

Once the hyperventilating stopped, Declan asked, "So...what are you guys going to do with her?"

"I guess she's coming to our house to sober up," replied Caleb.

"So...you guys are kidnapping her?" asked Declan.

"Uh…no. Where else can we take her? Safest thing to do is to take her home until she's conscious enough to call for someone to pick her up."

"And guess what, she's taking your room and you're sleeping on the couch," Keira said, beaming at Caleb.

"Why does she get to take my room? You're the one who demanded to take her with us. She should sleep in your room," Caleb replied defiantly.

"Caleb Miller! Are you suggesting that we should have just left this poor girl at a club where anything could have happened to her? You are unbelievable!" Keira once again sounded frighteningly like Declan's Aunt Jenny. Declan looked at Keira as his eyes widened and a trickle of sweat came down the side of his head.

Caleb answered quickly. "No, that's not what I'm suggesting, but why does it seem like you're blaming me for this?"

"Hey! We wouldn't be in this situation if you hadn't gotten her drunk. So man up and take some responsibility," demanded Keira once again sounding like Declan's aunt; Declan felt a small chill go down his back.

I can't imagine liking someone else more than Kiera, but if she's gonna turn into Aunt Jenny one day… thought Declan as he felt goose bumps form on his arms.

Keira and Caleb's argument continued all the way back to Declan's house to drop him off. Declan couldn't help but smile. *Only these two can bicker like that after a night like this.*

CHAPTER 8
-DECLAN-

Declan was sleeping when he heard a knocking sound on his window. *Maybe it's just my imagination*, he thought, but he heard it again.

He sat up and looked toward his window across the room from his bed, and he almost jumped when he saw someone standing outside his window. He rubbed his eyes to try to see a little more clearly and realized that it was Keira.

He walked up to his window and opened it. "Keira? What are you doing here?"

"I had to come see you, Deck. I want to talk about what happened today."

"Well, don't stand outside. Come on in. Are you still scared about the fight at the club?" asked Declan as she climbed through the window and into his room.

"No Deck, that's not what I wanted to talk about," she replied as she walked up close to Declan. He could feel the warmth of her body emanating from her even though they weren't touching yet.

"Oh ... um ... what did you want to talk about?" Declan swallowed hard, and his heart sped up.

"Us, Deck. I want to talk about us. Is there an 'us'? Is there ever going to be an 'us'?" She moved even closer, pressing up against Declan now, making him back up.

"Keira, I..." he stammered nervously. His heart pounded in his chest, and he noticed a certain part of his body wake up.

"Yes, Deck. What's the matter? You know how I feel about you. And I know how you feel about me. So...what's the problem?" Keira placed her hand on his cheek. The warmth of her hand on his cheek felt like a bolt of electricity running through his body, and his heart pounded even quicker.

"I've waited so long to tell you Keira. But I was afraid that I would..." Keira pulled his face down towards hers and placed her lips on his. He felt his world spin, he moved his right hand to the back of Keira's head and drew her in. Colors flashed in his field of vision like fireworks as they kissed. Declan thought that if there was heaven on earth then this moment would have been it.

His right hand moved down her back and he pulled her body against his. Both of his hands moved around to the front of her body and trailed upwards. All the way to the front of her neck, feeling every curve. His hands started to grip down tightly around her neck. He panicked and tried to stop, but it was as if his existence was trapped inside a body that he had no control over.

"Stop!" he screamed, but his body didn't react.

Choking sounds started to come out of Keira's mouth as she stared at Declan with fear. Declan looked into Keira's eyes and saw his own reflection. The grimace that was on his face reminded him of the look that was on his mother's face as she had tried to drown him.

೮೦೮ಚ

Declan jerked upright, screaming. He looked around his room for Keira but realized that it was just another nightmare in which he lost his sanity, and hurt someone he loved. He wanted to curl up into the fetal position for a while to recover from the horror that he had just experienced, but his head felt like it was being pounded like the bass drum of the Energizer Bunny. He wondered if it was because of the alcohol he drank the previous evening. Reaching over to his nightstand for his clock, he saw that it was nine o'clock. It had only been five hours since he went to bed. He tried to go back to sleep, but his headache seemed to be getting worse.

Maybe some water will help.

He sat up to look at the clock again. All of a sudden, it seemed to have floated its way into his hands. Declan shook his head and squeezed his eyes shut as he normally did when he thought that he saw something that was impossible.

What was in that liquor I drank last night?

He walked out of his room and into the kitchen. It was a small country-style kitchen with wooden benches and a table that his uncle carved. Declan felt the warm kitchen tiles against his feet as he entered. A smile crept up his face as the feeling brought back the memories of him and his uncle laying down the tiles together when he was ten. The stove was a gas stove that looked like it was from the fifties, but it made the most amazing pancakes, bacon, and eggs. Uncle Roy was sitting in the breakfast nook, reading the newspaper. Beams of sunlight shone through the window in the nook alighting Declan's uncle as if light was emanating from him. And as it was with every other morning, by the time Declan woke up, breakfast was already waiting for him. Seeing his uncle and being reminded of all the great times he had growing up in this house made Declan remorseful about the way he treated his uncle the previous evening.

"Morning, Deck," said Roy, not looking up from his newspaper. Declan opened the cabinet to pull out a glass, poured himself a glass of water, and sat down next to his uncle at the breakfast table.

"Morning, Uncle ... listen ... about yesterday ..." muttered Declan, but before he could finish, his uncle interrupted him by holding up a hand.

Roy looked up from his newspaper and said, "Deck, we're fine; don't worry about it."

"I was really out of line. I know that you care about me and you worry, so ... I'm sorry about the way I acted yesterday. You were just trying to help, and you didn't deserve that." Declan worried that his uncle would continue stonewalling him.

"Deck, I know that it's been hard for you. And if you need to vent once in a while, I can understand that," Roy replied warmly as he patted Declan on the shoulder.

A moment later, Aunt Jenny came out of her room and joined them at the breakfast table. Sitting down next to Roy, Jenny looked as if she was, at least, ten years younger than him; however, she was really ten months older. Jenny had a very unique look to her because she inherited her skin and hair color from her Chinese mother while she inherited blue eyes from her Texan father. Her eyes were an oddity since the darker pigments were usually dominant. This was the case with Declan, who inherited his mother's brown eyes while his father had the same blue eyes as his aunt.

"Mornin' Deck, are ya feelin' alright hon'? You look rather pale this mornin'." Aunt Jenny sounded concerned as she put on her glasses.

"Morning, Auntie, I'm fine. I just have a headache," replied Declan nervously.

"You came a runnin' home rather late last night..." Jenny said as she took a closer look at him. "Declan Peters, are you hung over? You answer me right quick young man!" demanded Jenny in her stern Texan accent.

"What? How did you—? Yes, and I'm sorry Auntie," admitted Declan. He could never lie to his aunt and uncle, not even as a little boy. It would literally pain him to ever see them hurt and to know that he hurt them would break his heart. More importantly, his aunt was an intimidating person. Although he loved her, he always wondered why someone as mellow and easy going as his uncle would have married someone like her.

"Your Daddy looked just like that there when he was hung over. Why, I remember when I was in high school. Ya daddy would come a sneakin' home in the middle of the night tuckered out after drinkin', and in the mornin' he would look just like ya did there right now." Aunt Jenny shook her head. She took a closer look at him, her glare faded. She smiled tenderly at Declan and took his hand. "I can't believe how much you look like your daddy. Sometimes lookin' at ya, makes me miss him so much. I know that you've never met ya old man, but the way you look, your personality, and how ya follow your heart is just like him. Except for ya eyes. You have ya mother's 'chinky' eyes."

Declan cringed, hearing his aunt use derogatory terms about race made him feel uncomfortable. Jenny felt that she had the right to use that term since she was half Chinese. But, he knew that she didn't use such terms to belittle a particular race. She simply thought that they painted a better picture of what she wanted to get across.

Despite his aunt's usage of the word "chinky," hearing about his father always made Declan smile. According to Aunt Jenny, his father, Jacob Peters, had been a very righteous man, after his rebellious teenage years. Whenever someone was in need, Declan's father would always put their needs before his own. "A true Christ Follower," said Aunt Jenny on many occasions. There were old news articles that Aunt Jenny had helped his father save a family out of a burning house and joined the volunteer group that helped rescue people after a hurricane. In the little town of Winter Garden, he had been somewhat of a local superhero. He suddenly and mysteriously died about two weeks before Declan was born.

"So...let's discuss the consequences of your act of underage drinkin'. You have to be a man and confess the thangs you've done, and whatever the consequence it brangs, ya gonna have to just accept it," said Jenny as she crossed her arms.

Declan's eyes widened, and he immediately went into panic mode. His aunt had always been very strict with him in terms of "consequences." When he had gotten into a fight in the fifth grade with Dewey Olson, she made him personally go over to Dewey's house to apologize to him and his parents. When he was thirteen, he succumbed to peer pressure and shoplifted a thumb drive from a computer store, and she made him take it back to the store and make a public apology over the store intercom. Luckily, the store manager didn't want to pursue shoplifting charges. Apparently, such drastic consequences were carried over from when Declan's grandparents were raising his father. According to his aunt, those were the drastic measures that groomed Declan's father into the righteous man that he was.

Droplets of sweat started to form on Declan's forehead. "Yes Auntie, I am willing to accept the consequences of my actions."

"Well, you committed a crime of underage drinking. Let's go pay the sheriff a visit and pray that he'll be willin' to give ya just a warnin'," Jenny declared as she started to get up from the table as if she was going to drag Declan to the sheriff's office immediately.

"Oh Jenny, give the boy a break. He was having a rough day…I told you last night about…" muttered Roy not willing to bring up the matter again in front of Declan.

"Ma sweet boy, alcohol is never an answer to problems. It will only make ya forget for a short period of time, but when ya wake up, the problem will still be there. And worse yet, you'll now have to deal with it with a poundin' headache." Jenny gave Declan a hug. "Well, I guess I can go easier on you this time only… hmm… you must have somehow fooled some alcohol vendor into selling the drinks to ya; I guess we'll start there with the apologies."

"No! We can't," exclaimed Declan as the events of last night came flooding back into his mind.

"Excuse me, young man. You just agreed that you would take responsibility there for your actions," Jenny said in shock. Declan was not someone who went back on his word. This made Jenny worry.

Reluctantly, Declan told his aunt and uncle about the events of the previous evening.

Amazed at what had gone on the previous night, Jenny said, "Praise the Lord that ya were there to save that girl last night. Who knows what coulda happened to her if ya guys weren't there."

"So...am I off the hook? I was a hero after all," Declan replied, putting on the most innocent face he could muster along with an angelic smile.

"Just because ya did a good deed doesn't cancel ya wrong doin's," said Jenny with a frown.

"Oh come on, Jenny, can we let him off the hook, just this once? You had already given him your word that you wouldn't make him go to the sheriff. And it seems that we can't go to this club either. Besides, the boy did a good thing, protecting that girl," pleaded Roy as he wrapped his arm around Jenny.

"Alright, alright. If only you could right a wrong by doin' a good deed after doin' a bad one, then we wouldn't need forgiveness. But fine, I'll let ya off the hook this one time. I want ya to go over to the Millers' right quick to check on the girl to make sure that she is alright. Ya are the reason that she's there after all. It is what a gentleman should do. Come on now. No time to waste; off ya go." Jenny waved him off.

Declan begrudgingly changed and left the house.

"What was that all about?" asked Roy, confused.

"That there boy is at an age where he should be datin'. What better way to start a relationship than bein' a knight in shining armor?" asked Jenny with a smirk on her face.

"Really? You want our boy to be dating a girl who gets drunk at bars?" Roy asked incredulously.

"Our boy is a good kid. Maybe bein' around our boy and the Millers will help lead the girl back to the straight and narrow. It's not the healthy that needs a doctor, but the sick."

"And that's why I love you. Stern and strict, but a heart of gold. I sure hope that being around our boy and the Millers can help that girl, but in terms of them dating, your efforts will be wasted. I think our boy already has a different girl in his heart."

CHAPTER 9
-DECLAN-

Declan quickly walked over to the Millers' house, not wanting to waste time since he had to be at work by noon. As he approached the door, it opened. Zoe was apparently leaving as Declan arrived.

Feeling a little awkward, Declan stammered, "Oh…a…hey…Zoe, right?"

Zoe gave Declan a strange but curious look before replying. "Yes, and who might you be?"

"Oh, I'm Declan. It's no wonder that you don't remember me. You were pretty drunk by the time I met you…Um…sorry, that didn't sound very good, and sorry my friend got you drunk," said Declan feeling awkward by the whole situation.

"So, you're Declan. I guess I owe you a thank you also. Thank you. I really must leave now," said Zoe hurriedly.

"Hey Deck," said Caleb as he walked Zoe out.

"Hey, Caleb. Are you going to drop Zoe off somewhere? You don't look so good. Are you hung over, too?" asked Declan as he studied Caleb's pale face.

"No worry boys, my ride's here." A limousine pulled up to the Millers' house. Zoe walked up to the limousine and the driver got out to open the door for her.

"How are you doing today, Miss ...," asked the driver as he looked down on his notepad, "Sullivan?" Zoe ignored the driver. Before she got into the limousine, she nodded at the two boys as a last sign of gratitude.

Caleb stared down the road even after the limo had turned the corner. "Wow, is she loaded or something?" Declan had never seen a limousine in his life.

"Did you watch the news this morning? Her parents were murdered here in Orlando. She was only here to identify their bodies last night. That's why she needed to get drunk."

"Oh wow...I can't imagine what it would be like to have to do that, but what does that have to do with my question?" asked Declan confused by his buddy's response.

"Dude, you didn't watch the news this morning then. She and her brother are the heirs to the Sullivan hotel chain," Caleb replied incredulously.

"Sullivan hotel chain? Never heard of it."

"Of course, you haven't. I guess my parents wouldn't have heard of it either. It is only the top of the line, super exclusive, super luxury, six-star hotel chain where even the rich can stay only through invitation." Caleb's voice was excited.

"Wow, that really is something," said Declan sarcastically.

"Just my type, hot and rich," said Caleb with a smirk apparently not realizing the sarcasm.

"You can stop drooling now. She's gone. What a bunch of pigs!" exclaimed Keira crossing her arms, standing in the doorway.

"I wasn't drooling," said Declan looking a little flustered.

"What, are you jealous? Why do chicks always hate other chicks that are hotter than them?" teased Caleb as he gave her a big grin.

"I am not jealous! I don't hate her!" Keira said defensively as her face reddened.

"Ah ha! So you're admitting that she's hotter than you," Caleb continued to tease as he pointed his index finger at her.

Keira fumed and walked back into the house, slamming the door behind her.

"Why do you always mess with her like that?" asked Declan as he smiled shaking his head.

"Oh, you won't understand unless you have a sibling," said Caleb still laughing.

"I mean, Zoe is hot, but I think Keira can hold her own," admitted Declan as his face reddened.

"Hey, that's my baby sister you're talking about! That's an area I don't want your mind anywhere near, okay?" Caleb tried to sound like an overly protective older brother, but then couldn't help but drop the demeanor and laugh.

Declan put up his hands and said, "It was just an observation."

"No observations about my sister. Got it," said Caleb trying to stay serious. Caleb always tried to put up a protective older brother front whenever there were guys around his sister. But he's never really stopped Keira from doing what she wanted; he simply couldn't.

"Alright, alright, I'll control my thoughts," replied Declan with a smirk.

Caleb walked toward the door and paused. "Want to join us for breakfast?"

"Sure, but I have to be at work by noon, though," replied Declan.

"No worries, Keira had already started making breakfast before Zoe said she had to go."

As they entered the house, Caleb yelled, "Is breakfast ready yet? What's taking so long? Deck has to leave for work soon."

"What am I, your servant? Both of you get your butts in here and help," demanded Keira.

They entered the kitchen and were amazed. There was a stack of pancakes about a foot high, a mountain of bacon and sausages, a plate of biscuits with a bowl of gravy, a plate of poached and sunny side up eggs, a tray of corned beef hash and muffins. Breakfast potatoes were baking in the oven, and a pitcher of freshly squeezed orange juice was sitting on the countertop.

"Whoa, I take back everything I said about you this morning. You are a goddess," said Caleb wide-eyed.

"Wow, this is a feast; how many people are you feeding?" said Declan still dazed by the spread of food.

"Oh, my small group is coming over for brunch in about half an hour," Keira replied without looking up as she continued her preparations.

"I thought you led a girls group?" asked Declan incredulously as he stared at the spread.

"Yeah, but they're all beastly jock chicks on her soccer team... like her," said Caleb with a mocking tone.

Keira glared at Caleb. "One more comment out of you about my friends, and you can get breakfast elsewhere. I thought you guys came in to help. Slice the fruit in that bowl. That's the last thing, and we can eat. And eat fast! My group is a girls only group. When my girls get here, you guys need to be gone."

Caleb and Declan quickly sliced all the fruit. Then they selected what they wanted to eat, buffet style in the kitchen, and gathered around the table in the breakfast nook to eat their breakfast.

"So Deck, I invited Zoe to our camping trip tomorrow. I figured that it might help her take her mind off things," said Caleb as he nonchalantly ate a strip of bacon.

"Why would she want to come with us? She just met us. Has she even gone camping before?"

"Hey, you told me that it was a boys-only trip this time when I asked if I could go," Keira reminded Caleb as she glared at him.

"It's only for boys...and hot girls, so you're going to have to stay home," teased Caleb, grinning at her.

Keira reached out and grabbed Caleb's plate of food.

"Alright, alright, you can come," Caleb laughed as he grabbed his plate back.

Keira grinned. "Neanderthals ... we can get you to agree to anything that involves food and women."

"Food ... good ... woman you cook good," said Caleb, sounding like a caveman.

"Hey, why do I always get lumped in with the bunch of men who are Neanderthals? I am a refined gentleman," said Declan cracking up as Caleb continued his caveman impressions.

"I don't think that all men are Neanderthals, just the boys who refuse to grow up as men," said Keira as she eyed Caleb with a smirk.

"What did the Neanderthals do to you that you have to lump them in with that?" said Declan as he pointed at Caleb.

"Good point; he is a race of his own!" exclaimed Keira with a large grin.

"Me no like the mocking," declared Caleb as he threw a poached egg at Declan. The perfectly cooked poached egg exploded on Declan's head and the gooey egg yolk seeped down his face.

"Oh, you are going down, cave man." Declan threw his sunny side up eggs back at him. Caleb was ready for the retaliation and dodged the incoming eggs, only to be hit in the face by a clump of corned beef hash thrown. He looked up to see where the projectile had come from. It was Keira with a surprised look on her face and one hand over her mouth.

Then an all-out food fight overtook the breakfast nook. When the fight was over, Declan had bacon, egg yolk, and corned beef hash in his hair and all over his face. Caleb was covered with orange juice and corned beef hash, and Keira had the bowl of sausage gravy dumped over her head.

"Oh my word, look at the mess in here! Good thing the rest of the food is still in the kitchen. I need to get cleaned up before the girls get here. Please clean up boys," said Keira as she ducked into the bathroom.

"Oh my word? When did you start saying that? You're becoming Mom!" shouted Caleb.

"I need to take a shower before going to work," said Declan running out of the house.

"Hey! Why am I left with the mess?" grunted Caleb.

CHAPTER 10
-TRISTAN AND ZOE-

"**W**here have you been?" asked Tristan, who was still in bed as he heard Zoe walk through the door of their hotel penthouse. The penthouse looked like a luxurious two-room apartment, with marble floors and crown molding throughout. All the decorative pieces were antiques, and the furniture had a Victorian theme.

"Nowhere, just out and about," replied Zoe in a shaky tone as she took off her boots.

"You don't look so good. What happened?" asked Tristan as he walked out of his room and into the living room of the penthouse.

Zoe sighed as she walked quickly into her bedroom and sat on her bed, trying to avoid the conversation. "I went to a club for a few drinks. I got drunk and passed out. Can we talk about this later? I'm tired."

"You got drunk at a club? Are you okay? Did anything happen?" Tristan followed Zoe into her room, showing concern.

"Nothing ... happened, I'm fine."

"You don't look fine. I know that you like to think that we're invincible, but look what happened to Mom and Dad; we have to be careful." Tristan stared hard into Zoe's eyes. The mental image of their parents turning into a pile of bones came flooding back into Zoe's head.

"We're not the same as Mom and Dad, now are we?" Zoe defiantly shook her head to rid herself of the mental image.

"No, we're not...I don't know what we are," Tristan replied sounding a little angry.

"So...where do we go from here?" asked Zoe as she leaned back on the bed. The smooth comforter from the bed enveloped her back, and she wanted to turn over and bury her face in it as she felt tears welling up in her eyes.

"We continue living our lives. Do what we always do," declared Tristan, sitting down next to Zoe.

"But why did they have to lie?" Tears threatened to flow as Zoe asked this question.

"I don't know, but we can find out," said Tristan reassuringly, as he placed a hand on Zoe's.

"Find out? How? Do I just go to *Google* and look it up? Sure, let's just type in all our abilities on the search bar and see if anything turns up," Zoe said sarcastically, pulling her hand away from Tristan as she turned her face to hide her tears. Zoe thought back on all the strange things that they had seen over the years, all the different creatures of the night that they had met. All of them had some sort of demonic origin.

"We've been hunting down demons ever since we were teenagers. We haven't been the only ones. Think of the other groups we've been competing with. I bet they would know more about demons. We can seek out the hunters, the exorcists, or the fae, someone...anyone. Who knows, maybe Mom and Dad were captured. If we can find out who captured them, then we can find them and demand answers." Tristan walked over to the window, looking out.

"Maybe I just want to forget everything that Mom and Dad taught me. Like you said, they lied to us. I don't know what to believe anymore, and I just want to be normal. We grew up believing that we descended from angels and hunted down demons. That was in no way a normal childhood. Haven't you ever wanted to just be normal? I've thought about that so many times as we were growing up." Zoe stood face to face with him and was angry. "We were taught that humans were below us and not worth our time. I didn't have friends. I didn't even go to the prom. I just wanted to grow up like everyone else."

"Go to the prom? Why do you care so much about being human all of a sudden? Humans are so frail and weak. What do they have to offer us?" Tristan sounded puzzled by Zoe's sudden fascination.

"We're half-human, first of all. And they're not weak. A bunch of humans risked their lives for me last night. And after having some decent conversations with them this morning, I think that I might even consider them friends." Zoe suddenly turned away from him and crumpled on her bed.

"You made 'friends' with humans?" Tristan asked with disgust. "What do you mean, they risked their lives for you? I thought you said nothing happened." Tristan walked over to Zoe and asked, "What happened last night?"

"I told you, I was at a club and I was drunk!" exclaimed Zoe not wanting to say more.

"And then…?" Tristan prompted as he sat down on her bed.

"The club owner tried to take advantage of me, but a bunch of humans protected me," responded Zoe sounding a little defeated as she buried her face once again. Zoe had always depended on her own strength and power to protect herself. Hearing herself say that someone else had protected her nearly destroyed her self-image. And worst of all, those who had protected her were humans. The humans that her parents taught her were weak and selfish. They were the same humans who were said to be only concerned about personal gains and were not to be trusted. It was as if her entire world came crumbling down.

Rage burned within Tristan's chest. He slammed his fist so hard on the side table that it exploded into splinters. "Did you kill him?" he demanded with menace in his eyes.

"I was drunk; I could barely even take in what was going on. Besides, what was I to do? Reveal my abilities in front of a club full of humans?"

"Where was this club? No one tries anything on you and gets away with it!" declared Tristan with murder in his eyes.

"Trist, pipe down... you need to keep your head level. I think the club owner was demon-possessed. He moved in a way that I've never seen humans move before. As a matter of fact, I don't even think that I've seen a demon move that quickly. I want some payback, too, but we have to be smart about it."

"How did a bunch of humans protect you from a demon?" asked Tristan intrigued. *If these humans discovered what we are, I might have to eliminate them*, he thought.

"I'm not sure. I wasn't conscious through most of it," Zoe replied, ashamed.

"Hmm... I'll deal with those humans later. We have ourselves a demon to catch," said Tristan with a smirk on his face, "and torture."

CHAPTER 11
-DECLAN-

Declan was glad that Caleb had come back from college. At first, he was worried that Caleb would go on and on about college like he did on the phone, but when they were together, it seemed just like old times in high school. Declan had been sulking for the past couple months, being resentful that the whole world seemed to have moved on without him. *Everyone was having new exciting adventures after high school, like going to college, traveling, Peace Corps, or moving to a different city. But nope, not me! I had to stay behind to help out with my family.* He would say to himself.

Getting to spend time with his friends once again melted away Declan's resentment. And now, he felt reenergized as he walked into work. With a new spring in his step, Declan entered the elevator and pressed the button for the third floor.

"Wait, please," said a voice as a hand shot through the doors before they closed all the way.

Declan quickly pounded the "open door" button on the elevator panel. "Sorry about that! I didn't see you coming," Declan apologetically said as an old man in a white UAP uniform, like his own, walked into the elevator. He had a full head of white hair cut in a GI style. His black piercing eyes looked sharp and alert, despite the relaxed demeanor, the rest of his body showed. Although the old man looked like he was in his sixties, his movements were swift and agile like that of someone much younger.

For an old man, he has an extremely muscular build, Declan thought.

"Oh that's okay, I made it in. Hi, I'm Victor. Today's my first day working here." Victor extended his hand for a handshake.

"Hi, I'm Declan. Which floor?" asked Declan as he shook Victor's hand.

"Eighth floor, please. I'm supposed to report to the admin office before going to the third where they assigned me," Victor replied with a big smile on his face.

"Oh, cool! I also work on the third floor. I guess I'll be seeing you around."

As they talked, the elevator doors opened up, and Declan walked out while Victor continued up to the eighth floor. Declan saw Joe and walked up to greet him. "Good Morning! How are you?" Declan asked in a cheerful tone.

"It's a beautiful day, but not as beautiful as me," said Joe in his Johnny Bravo voice and continued, "You seem chipper."

"Just excited about my camping trip tomorrow." Declan rolled his eyes excitedly.

"Oh, I see. Where are you guys planning to go camping?"

"Just up in Lake Louisa, not too far," replied Declan, thankful that Joe was dropping the Johnny Bravo act. He hated that cartoon growing up.

"Oh, I see, that's just in Clermont right?" asked Joe squinting his eyes and looking up involuntarily as he normally did when he was thinking.

"Yeah, Caleb, Keira, and I have been going camping up in Lake Louisa since we were kids. We'd do the hike in the morning, then we'd rent a canoe to go out into the middle of the lake to fish. And at night, we'd eat whatever we caught; sometimes we didn't catch anything, so we'd bring backup canned food," responded Declan with a smile on his face.

It would just be like old times, he told himself.

"By the way, who was that with you when you came out of the elevator?"

"Oh, he said his name was Victor. Today's his first day. Why do you have your thinking face on?" Declan asked, raising an eyebrow.

"Hmm ... Victor ... he looks familiar. I know that I've seen him before, just can't remember when."

"I know that you're getting old, but ... senility seems a little premature," mocked Declan as he laughed. "He's probably been around the industry for a while. I mean, he's kind of old ... you don't just decide one day when you're close to retirement to go work at a behavioral hospital." Declan waved off Joe's suspicion.

"Hey, hey, watch the 'O' word. If you let Rosy hear you using that word, she'll probably knock you on the back of your head," said Joe with a smirk. Joe had learned his lesson. Rosy might be motherly, but she was not to be crossed.

"I heard my name. Are you boys talking about me behind my back?" declared Rosy with a stern look on her face, which made her crow's feet even darker.

The two jumped slightly and said, "No ma'am!"

"I didn't think so. Don't you boys have work to do?" Rosy asked as she tapped her foot.

"Yes, ma'am," they both answered as they hurried off, not wanting to risk becoming the vomit cleaning specialist for the next month.

ಬಅಚಿ

Declan spent the rest of the afternoon helping the nurses escort the patients to and from their rooms. He also sat down with a few of the patients for some very interesting conversations about UFOs, vampires, and government conspiracies as he delivered their food. He had to have some of these conversations discretely, as the doctors didn't like the staff encouraging such thoughts with the patients. It wasn't until around 5:00 o'clock that Declan ran into Victor again.

"Hey Victor, so how's your first day so far?" asked Declan.

"Oh, it's been fine. Quiet," replied Victor, sounding almost disappointed.

"So… Victor, where did you work before coming here?"

"Oh, I worked everywhere. I'm a freelancer, so I just accept contracts here and there when the hospitals need the extra manpower. Most of the time, I get calls from hospitals in the Southeast region. Whenever they need the extra muscle, I'm there to offer my services." Victor flexed his biceps. Declan cringed, but quickly hid it so as not to be rude.

Why are old people around this center always so strange? Declan thought.

"You're hired muscle?" responded Declan incredulously, but then he realized he had crossed the ambiguous line between curiosity and rudeness. He quickly said, "I mean … I'm sorry, I just haven't met anyone else who was doing that at your—"

"Hey I wasn't always sixty-three years old; I've been doing this since I was about your age," said Victor.

Declan thought to himself with horror in his eyes, *Oh my God, this is my future? NO!* He imagined himself working at the center in his sixties as a strange muscular old man flexing his muscles in front of people. The horror must have been too apparent because the old man clapped him on the back. "Declan? Declan? Hey there kid, are you okay? You kind of blanked out for a moment."

"I'm sorry, I was just thinking about something." Declan swallowed hard, still horrified.

"I'm actually surprised that I was called in when things are so calm around here," Victor said as he looked around.

"Well, we're on the third floor. The older patients are on other floors, and more severe cases are usually on the fifth. Yesterday, we got this new patient who seemed all right one minute and then got really violent the next. If we hadn't restrained him in time, he could have really hurt the pastor. Since then, he's been moved to the fifth floor. Don't know what got into him; he was supposed to have been suffering from anorexia, but it seems like he's suffering from much more than that." Declan quickly shut up as he realized that he sounded like a gossiper.

"He got very violent with the pastor, you say? Any other strange things you noticed about this patient ... wild eye movements or strange smells?" Victor asked with excitement in his eyes.

"Hmm ... yes now that you mention it, there was something strange. His body language was somewhat ... contradictory. He had the wild eye movements that you mentioned, but his body looked to be completely at rest. And strange smells?" Declan shrugged.

"Yes, like the smell of sulfur," replied Victor with a serious look.

"Sulfur? What does sulfur smell like?" asked Declan confused now.

"Like ... you know ... rotten eggs ... fart ...," replied Victor impatiently.

Declan couldn't help but burst out with laughter. "You almost got me there. Farts! That's hilarious."

"Oh... yes, ha-ha, it was just a fart joke." Victor forced a smile and then continued. "So ... did it seem like he was particularly gassy?"

"Um... not that I noticed," replied Declan, trying hard to stop laughing.

"Well, it seems to be rather calm here. Maybe I should take a look around the fifth floor and offer them my services," responded Victor turning toward the elevator.

"You actually want to seek out violent patients? That's messed up," said Declan incredulously.

"It keeps me feeling young! What fun would moving from city to city be if I didn't get a little action along with it?" replied Victor with a smirk on his face.

If traveling UAPs get to move to a different city for work every so often, then I want to be one too, he thought.

CHAPTER 12
-TRISTAN AND ZOE-

"**A**re you sure you're ready for this?" asked Tristan as he and Zoe huddled outside of club Matrix.

"I'm always ready to kick some demon butt," Zoe replied smugly.

"Alright, then let's go. Try to stall for a few minutes; it's going to take me a while to figure out the piping."

Zoe walked around the building and into club Matrix through the backdoor. As soon as Zoe disappeared around the corner, Tristan jumped up towards the building and grabbed hold of the gutter that ran along the roofline. He pulled himself up from there and climbed onto the roof of the building.

Zoe could hear sounds coming from the main lobby where the dance floor was located, so she snuck in slowly to make sure that no one saw her. She peeked out and saw some of the staff tidying up the place. The bartender was setting out the liquor, and the DJ was plugging cables into different sound equipment. She didn't see Owen, though.

The place looked different during the daytime compared to how it looked the previous night. The strobe light, fog machines, and loud music had covered up what was now an empty, dirty warehouse. The couches that the clubbers lounged on were stained. Traces of beer, make up, and vomit could easily be spotted in the now well-lit space. Broken glass was strewn across the dance floor.

Wow, I was really slumming it last night, thought Zoe as she almost gagged. Shaking her head to pull her attention away from her disgust of the club, she took note of the staff present. *There are too many humans around. I'm going to have to do something about them.*

She continued to observe and realized that the staff was constantly going into the storage room to retrieve items. She quickly followed a young girl into the storage room. Walking right up behind her, Zoe moved her lips against her ear and whispered, "Sleep." The girl slowly sat down on the floor and closed her eyes. Within five seconds, she was in a deep sleep.

Just the right touch, she thought. Being able to push her will onto someone else by speaking was a special talent that was unique to Zoe. It was a talent that had manifested over the past year. Zoe first noticed it when she was in Rome earlier that year, and her purse got snatched. While pursuing the thief into a back alley, she yelled at him to stop. To her surprise, the thief's arms and legs stopped stiff and his momentum carried him tumbling down. When she reached him, he was still stuck in a running pose on the ground ... dead. Apparently, when she yelled at him to stop, everything in his body stopped, including his heart. After testing her ability out for several months, she learned to be very careful with her words, and the softer she spoke the less drastic were the effects.

Zoe stayed hidden in the storage room. Every time someone went in, they didn't come out. Thinking that she had gotten the entire staff locked up in the storage room, Zoe walked out into the main lobby of the club. She quickly realized that she had forgotten about the bouncers who had just arrived to work.

Time to tumble with Tweedledee and Tweedledum, she thought.

"Hey, you're that drunk chick from last night," said Buck.

"That's right, boys, and I've come for some payback." Zoe rushed at them with rage and all they saw was a blur. She sent Charlie flying back a couple of feet as her punch landed on his abdominal region, and as Buck tried to restrain her from behind, she tossed him over her head and into Charlie.

Zoe was planning to continue bashing the two bouncers but she heard sounds of clapping behind her.

"Quite a show you're putting on. I was going to look for you, but it seems that you just couldn't get enough of me," Owen said as he looked at Zoe from the bottom up and whistled. "We are going to have so much fun together."

"I'm sure it's going to be more fun for me than you," Zoe said as she rushed at Owen with a combination of punches and kicks. Owen dodged a few punches and blocked a few kicks rather effortlessly, but had a surprised expression on his face.

"You're a demon. What business do you have with me?" asked Owen with a serious face after jumping back, away from Zoe.

"Who are you calling a demon? You … demon! I'm here for some payback for last night," responded Zoe angrily.

"I apologize for last night; I had no idea that you were a demon."

"I am not a demon!" yelled Zoe as she charged him with more speed and power than before.

Owen caught one of Zoe's arms and held her in a lock. "Enough of this, there is no point in this fight; you will not win. If you leave now, I will pretend nothing happened, and I won't pursue you."

"Take your hands off my sister, demon!" yelled Tristan as he ran so fast that it looked like he was there one second and somewhere else the next. He punched Owen in the face. Owen let go of Zoe and skidded back a couple feet.

Two demons, thought Owen as he recovered from Tristan's punch.

Tristan and Zoe both attacked at the same time. Owen continued to dodge and block, now putting a little more effort into it. Tristan was not able to get in another blow. Just as Tristan was thinking of the next attack, Owen grabbed him by the arm and threw him across the room. Zoe tried to get a blow in midway during Owen's throw to catch him off-guard, but her punch was intercepted by Owen's knee as he raised it to block her. Then he kicked her and she flew across the room.

"Seeing your skill level, I can tell that you are just a pair of possessed teens. You should leave now before I change my mind and really put the hurt on you," threatened Owen, staring at the two as if they were pests.

"I'm going to tear that smug look off your face!" Tristan took out a little device and pushed the button on it. The device set off an incendiary directly underneath one of the sprinklers; all the sprinklers in the club activated, and it was if it was raining throughout the entire club.

Owen's strength started to drain away with the water running down his body. "Now why'd you have to go and do that? So you want to go two against one without powers? Do you think that your bodies will hold up before you defeat me?"

"Who said anything about going against you without powers? Like I said before, I'm not a demon," Zoe replied as she zoomed past Tristan and behind Owen, restraining him. "I'm just going to hold you here until all your powers have dwindled away, and you're nothing but a pile of bones." Zoe pressed his head down on the ground, which now had about an inch of water.

Owen started to laugh. "Oh, I can't believe it. I didn't think that there were any of you around. It has been forbidden for so many years." Owen's voice sounded different than when he had spoken before.

"His body isn't decaying!" yelled Tristan in an unsure tone.

Owen laughed even louder. "You kids really don't know anything, do you? My body won't decay because my host is still alive; I don't do the whole possession thing."

"You're speaking through your human host right now, demon. What do you call this if it's not possession?" asked Zoe.

"You've never heard of channeling?" asked Owen incredulously. "I lend my powers to my host, and he allows me to interact with the world through him. It's a rather nice symbiotic relationship. But enough with the Demonology 101. Who made you?" Owen said in a scratchy sinister voice.

"What do you mean, 'who made us?'" asked Zoe, sounding offended.

With that, Owen gave another maniacal laugh. "You're a fluke of nature! You're just a byproduct of possession. Which low life traitorous demon spawned you two?"

"You're not in any position to ask questions. And don't talk about our parents that way," Tristan demanded as he punched Owen in the face and continued with a few kicks to the ribs. Zoe heard the cracks as Owen's ribs broke. "I'll be asking the questions, or there're plenty more where that came from," Tristan sneered.

"What do you want to know? My broken ribs have punctured my lungs; you'll need to get me out of the running water so that I can heal. Otherwise, you're not going to be able to get much out of me," stammered Owen with his own voice.

"First of all, give us your name," Tristan demanded, pulling Owen's head to face him.

"Owen, my name is Owen!" Tristan kicked him in the ribs one more time.

"Not your host's name, demon, what is your name? And don't lie to me because I wouldn't think twice about putting you into a box and throwing it into the middle of the ocean" Tristan grinned menacingly at him.

"Vetis, my demon's name is Vetis. Please, I need to heal," stammered Owen in his own voice.

"What do you mean byproduct of possession?" asked Zoe. Owen tried to speak but coughed up a few mouthfuls of blood. Tristan then dragged Owen out of the water.

Just as Owen's upper body was out of the reach of the sprinklers, Owen opened his mouth and a writhing black shadow shot out. Tristan jumped back in surprise as he didn't expect the demon to abandon its host so quickly, considering the whole symbiotic relationship it just preached. The shade crashed against the startled Tristan, knocking him down. It then ran off. Zoe chased after the shade and grabbed at its leg, preventing the demon from escaping.

Tristan watched in surprise. *How in the world is she holding it in place like that?* He focused his sight onto Zoe and saw the light inside of Zoe that represented her life force. The longer Zoe held onto the shade the more the light seemed to fade.

Tristan screamed, "Stop Zoe! Don't do it." He rushed over to Zoe to sever her connection with the demon. Vetis disappeared into the shadows in the corner of the room.

"Damn it! He escaped!" exclaimed Tristan as he tried to chase the shade without success. He looked back at Zoe and noticed that she was glaring at him.

"Zoe, how did you hold the demon in its spirit form like that?" he asked still amazed at what she had done.

"I used my brain! I noticed that every time a demon tried to get into one of us, it couldn't penetrate and always ended up shoving us aside. I figured that we should, therefore, also be able to interact with it. Why'd you stop me?" Zoe stared angrily at Tristan. "You heard him; he knew what we were."

"I was watching you as you held the demon. Whatever it is that allows our physical bodies to interact with the spiritual bodies of the demons uses up our life force. I saw your life force dimming as you held on. Zoe! That should only be used as a last resort! I know you want answers, but it's not worth throwing your life away." Tristan's shouting matched Zoe's anger.

Was I really about to force that demon into myself to get some answers? Am I really that desperate to find out, that I would risk my life to do it? Her anger drained out of her as she reflected on her actions.

"A byproduct of possession… we were just a byproduct … a fluke," Zoe crumbled to the floor, warm tears filling her eyes.

"He's a demon, Zoe. Demons lie!" He walked over to Zoe, pulling her up. "Let's search out other demons and see if their stories match."

"No Tristan, I need to get my mind off things. Can we please be demon-free for a while? I don't know how far I might go the next time we encounter a demon." A tear escaped out of the corner of Zoe's right eye.

Tristan held his sister as she sobbed. "Well ... how do you want to get your mind off things?" he asked.

Zoe thought about it and replied, "Remember those humans I told you about?"

CHAPTER 13
-DECLAN-

Declan was eating breakfast with his aunt and uncle in the breakfast nook when the sound of a car horn interrupted them. "Caleb and Keira are here. I've gotta get going," said Declan as he excused himself from the breakfast table. He grabbed his bag and tent as he rushed out of the house.

Roy looked at Jenny and shook his head as he smiled. "Deck acts like a kid anxiously waiting for a play date when he's around those two."

Jenny placed her hand on Roy's and smiled. "That boy might think he's a grown man, but he'll always be just a kid."

Excitedly, Declan walked up to Caleb's car. The car was a white Toyota Prius with a hatchback. Declan had many great memories with Caleb in that car. Once, they ventured off on a road trip across the state to Panama City during spring break of their senior year. Declan looked forward to the new adventures they would have on this trip. When he looked into the car, it wasn't just Caleb and Keira in the car like he expected. In the backseat were Zoe and another guy around his age. The guy had a lot of similar features as Zoe, tanned flawless skin, black hair, and dark empty eyes that somehow unnerved him. Declan knew that this must be Zoe's twin brother.

Caleb stuck his head out of the driver's window and yelled out, "Hey Deck, you won't need your tent this time. Since we have so many people, we decided to just rent one of their cabins." He pulled the lever to pop open the trunk.

"Hey, you never know when a tent can come in handy," said Declan as he peered into the trunk and found a small spot, just enough for his bag.

"Sorry dude, no space!" yelled Caleb.

Declan quickly ran back into his house to ditch the tent, and as he ran back out, Keira got out of the passenger side of the car. "Zoe, would you like to sit in the front with Caleb? I'd like to sit in the back with Declan."

"Oh… okay," replied Zoe, giving Tristan a nervous glance.

Keira opened the door to the backseat to let Zoe out. As Zoe got out of the backseat, she looked back at Tristan and mouthed the word "behave."

Keira looked at Tristan and said, "I'll sit in the middle since you boys are taller." Keira moved into the backseat with her thigh touching Tristan's. The backseat of the Prius would barely fit the three of them, so they had to squeeze together.

Tristan looked a little uncomfortable with her sitting so close to him and decided to look away. He wasn't used to being so close to a girl. Although there were many girls during high school that had a crush on him, he always kept to himself just as his parents asked him to do during his teen years. And before that, girls had coodies that he didn't want. Besides, he was always taught that humans were beneath them and didn't deserve their attention.

"Hey guys! You must be Zoe's brother right? Hi, I'm Declan," Declan said as he climbed into the back seat.

"Hi, I'm Tristan. Nice to meet you. It was kind for you guys to let us come along on your trip." *What am I doing in a car with these dumb humans? If it wasn't for Zoe, I would never … This is going to be a long day …*

The two shook hands, and Tristan quickly turned his head back toward the window.

"The more the merrier," said Keira cheerfully and padded Tristan on the knee.

Tristan almost flinched, but acted as if nothing had happened. *Filthy humans,* he thought; his cheeks reddened slightly.

"I believe the thanks was directed to Declan and me; remember this was supposed to have been a boys-only trip," said Caleb mockingly.

"Why did you want a boys-only trip this year? We always go on trips together," Keira demanded, sticking her tongue out at Caleb knowing that he could see her through the rearview mirror.

"There are just things that Declan and I can talk about without having to worry about being overheard by girls... especially annoying little baby sisters." Caleb turned his head and stuck his tongue out at Keira through the mirror.

Declan yelled out. "Keep your eyes on the road, dude!"

"Ooooh, like I'm even interested in what boys have to say anyway. It's usually some dumb perverted comment about girls, who gives," Keira replied, making another face at Caleb.

"Do you guys always bicker like this?" asked Tristan, feeling very uncomfortable with the situation.

Both Declan and Zoe said, "Yes," at the same time and laughed.

"I had to endure two hours of it yesterday morning," said Zoe in a joking manner.

Keira and Caleb both blushed and remained silent.

"It's just their dynamics; you'll get used to it. It's actually quite entertaining to watch," chided Declan with a big grin on his face.

"Well then, sit back, relax, and enjoy the show," said Caleb as they drove off.

ഔഃയ

The group arrived at Lake Louisa State Park and checked into their cabin. The cabin was cozy and right off of the lake. The front porch had a few chairs and benches that allowed people to hang out and watch the water. There were wooden floors throughout the cabin, and it was warmly furnished with wooden furniture. The kitchen had all the equipment needed to make a decent meal and the dining room had a long table that allowed for ten people. There were two bedrooms that contained two queen beds and a sleeper sofa.

"Wow, this cabin is wonderful. It feels so comfy," said Keira as she twirled around the cabin. Declan couldn't help but watch.

"Yeah, don't know why we didn't try one of these before," Caleb said as he checked out the rooms and sat down on one of the beds.

"Yeah, surprisingly, it doesn't even smell like a cabin." Declan had stayed in cabins before when his uncle or Joe took him hunting. Most of the time, all they were able to afford were really small old cabins that had a distinct smell of moldy wood.

Is this a joke? This is just a shack ... right? Thought Zoe.

I'm stuck in a dump with a bunch of humans ... oh great ... thought Tristan as he rolled his eyes at the girl twirling in front of him, but felt his heart quicken as he watched.

The group brought in all their bags and started to unpack their stuff. Caleb and Declan took one bedroom; Zoe and Keira took another, leaving Tristan the sleeper sofa. Caleb brought a box in from his car and took it into the kitchen.

"So what kind of food did you bring?" asked Declan suspiciously eyeing the gigantic box that Caleb was carrying.

Caleb opened up the box, and it was filled with liquor, from Vodka to Tequila and different fruit juices for mixing.

"That's not going to feed us when we're hungry," replied Declan disappointed as he dug through the box.

"What happened to the box of food I packed last night?" asked Keira as she glared at Caleb.

"Oh, I figured my box was better, and there was limited trunk space. So, it was left in the garage," Caleb replied with a smirk.

"You did what! You could have at least put the food back in the refrigerator. Now's it's gonna go bad in the garage!" yelled Keira in disbelief.

"Alcohol! That's what I'm talking about," said Zoe, cheerful for the first time in days. Completely ignoring the altercation, she reached into the box to pull out a bottle of Vodka. A hand reached out and stopped her.

"Do you have a problem you would like to discuss with me?" asked Tristan as he held her arm firmly, but Zoe shrugged him off.

"Seriously, Caleb, what are we going to eat tonight?" Keira's voice trembled in anger.

"Sorry to rain on your parade, but dude, we need grub," Declan said while shaking his head.

"Don't worry, we'll catch some fish later," declared Caleb nonchalantly.

How is he always so carefree? Why couldn't I be like that? Thought Declan.

"Caleb, you are such a —," yelled Keira,

"Well, shall we go for a hike first or try our luck with the lake to see if we can catch some fish for dinner?" Declan injected, trying to prevent a fight.

"I'm really not a big fan of hiking…" Zoe winced as she thought about the potential mosquito bites.

"Great! Then let's go canoeing and fishing," Declan suggested, trying to cheer everyone up.

CHAPTER 14
-KEIRA-

Park Ranger Nelly had just returned to work at Louisa Lake State Park from medical leave. The park ranger was a gentleman in his late fifties, about five-feet-six-inches in height with black hair and a tinge of grey on the sideburns. He recently had to get a few freckles and moles removed from his neck because the doctors had found some cancer cells. Now, he was more conscientious about sun exposure than ever. As he was examining his face in the mirror to see if he had gotten more freckles, Keira walked into the ranger's station.

It was a tidy little cabin with a desk in the middle of the foyer. Around the corner of the foyer were a living room and a hallway that led to the sleeping quarters. Although it was available for use for all the park rangers, Nelly had put his finishing touches on all the furniture in the station so that it felt more like home.

"Good morning, Ranger Nelly. How are you doing today?" asked Keira with her big bright blue eyes flashing.

"Well, if it isn't Keira. I'm just dandy. Had to get some freckles and moles removed due to skin cancer, but they removed all of it. I should be square if it doesn't come back. I hope…" Nelly replied. Unsure of why he had brought that up, he shook his head and looked at Keira.

Keira placed her hand on his. "Oh wow, sorry you had to go through that, and I'm glad you're okay. That must have been scary to go through," Keira said, as her eye watered up. Nelly stared into Keira's watery eyes and felt comforted.

"Yeah, I didn't know what to think when the doctors told me that it was cancer. They tried to assure me that the type of cancer I had was fairly common in Florida since we have so much sun exposure. But, cancer is cancer! So … yeah, I hope it doesn't come back because if it does they tell me that it can be more aggressive than the last time."

"Yikes! I thought you had a more serious and somewhat nervous look on your face when I walked in." She sympathized as she gave his hand a small squeeze. She noticed that the poor ranger was so distracted by the situation that he had barely touched his breakfast sandwich on the table. "Don't forget to eat your breakfast! Some food in your system should do you good."

"Oh, I just haven't had much of an appetite ever since. Just don't know what I'll do if the cancer comes back!" Nelly said with his head down.

"Do you know what the chances are of it coming back? Are there any preventative measures you can take?"

Nelly sighed. "There aren't any conclusive studies about the likelihood of it coming back, but I've been more conscious of using sunblock and I only go into the sun when I have to. Gosh, I wish someone had taught us about the damage the sun can have on our skin when I was your age. Sunblock didn't even exist! There really isn't much else I can do now but just sit here and worry about it." Nelly paused a moment and said with a laugh, "Gee, I sound like a sunblock infomercial,"

Keira gave him a smile. "Nelly, I'm sure everything will turn out okay. I mean, there are things that we can control and there are things that we can't. For those things that we can't, it's easier to just surrender them over to God, rather than worry about something that we can't do anything about. Right?" Keira gave his hand a reassuring squeeze. "Would you mind if I prayed for you?"

"I'm not sure how that would really help me... sorry, I know you mean well, but I'm just not into that," replied Nelly trying to sound polite; he pulled his hand away.

"That's okay, I'll still keep you in my prayers," Keira said sounding a little disappointed.

Nelly tried to break the awkwardness. "So... are you here with Caleb and Declan again?" He looked out the window to see who she was with.

"We've brought some new friends this year. I think we'll need an extra canoe this time ... unless you have an even bigger one," Keira teased.

"Are you kidding me? You guys use the biggest canoe we have every time you come. Next size up would be a barge. So ... it'll be the big canoe and a standard canoe this time. Just go around the back and pick out the two you want."

"Thanks, Nelly. We'll see you around." Keira was about to exit but noticed Nelly quickly turning back to his mirror. "Nelly, put down that mirror and stop worrying. And eat your breakfast!"

"Alright, try not to get into trouble. And wear some sunblock!" he shouted back.

Nelly went back to examining his face for freckles, and after a few minutes, he smelled something strange. He looked down at the sandwich in front of him. *This egg sandwich couldn't have gone bad that quickly.*

ℂℂℂ

"Are you guys sure you don't want to borrow one of our fishing rods?" Keira asked as she raised an eyebrow at the two Sullivan siblings.

"Nah, we'll be fine without it. We'll just spear the fish using some branches," Tristan replied nonchalantly.

"Really? That's kind of awesome!" exclaimed Declan incredulously.

"I'll believe it when I see it," Caleb said cynically as he crossed his arms.

"It doesn't look that hard. I've seen it on TV so many times. I'm sure we can do it" Zoe was confident.

"Well, let's get going then!" Caleb loved a challenge.

The group set off into Lake Louisa. Lake Louisa was one of the largest of the 13 chain lakes in the area. The water in the lake was so clear that it was one of the few lakes that were preferred by swimmers. Declan, Caleb, and Keira were in the big canoe while Tristan and Zoe took the other one.

The sunray glinted off the shiny waters, and Declan couldn't help but smile. He felt the warm sunrays across his body as the cool breeze blew on him. The rocking motion of the canoe relaxed him. He loved spending time at the lake with his two best friends and missed doing so over the past several months. Now being in a canoe with them, felt just like old times.

They rowed their canoes out into the middle of the lake and Declan and Caleb baited their fishing hooks with little bits of sausage and dropped them into the water. Tristan and Zoe stood up in their canoe and held their long branches up as if they were ready to stab into the water.

Glancing over to Zoe and Tristan's canoe, Keira asked, "Do you guys see any fish?"

Caleb smirked. "Even if you could see the fish, you wouldn't be able to tell how deep under the surface the fish really are."

"Are these guys for real?" Keira asked laughing.

"They look serious to me. I mean look at them. If I tried standing up in our canoe we'd probably flip over. Somehow they're keeping their canoe balanced," Declan responded with a confused look on his face. The three laughed as they watched how serious the two Sullivans looked with their spear ready pose.

Keira, Declan, and Caleb jumped when Tristan suddenly threw his branch into the water. Tristan's face then relaxed and formed a look of smugness.

"Nice shot!" cheered Zoe without moving her eyes from the water.

The other three looked confused. Suddenly, Tristan's branch floated back up to the surface and at the end of the branch a fish was impaled. The threesome dropped their jaws.

"Caught one," Tristan said smugly.

Without any notice, Zoe launched her branch into the water. The other three jumped again. They leaned over the side of their canoe and watched as Zoe's branch floated up with a fish caught on the end of it. They looked over at the other canoe with amazement.

"I think my fish is bigger," said Zoe with a smirk on her face.

"That just means that your fish was easier to spear. I don't know why you feel like bragging about that," Tristan replied mockingly.

Zoe's smirk turned into a frown. "Oh, I guess you're right."

The rest of the fishing trip turned out to be a competition for spearing the smallest fish for the Sullivan siblings, which was no value added for dinner. Luckily, Declan, Keira, and Caleb each caught a largemouth bass over twenty inches in length and a few crappies, otherwise, they might have had to go out and buy dinner.

⁐ℙℂℂ

"Wow, that smells really good," exclaimed Declan looking over Keira's shoulder to look at the fish cooking on the grill.

"Nothing like cooking fresh items on an open fire. Good thing some previous visitor left these spices in the kitchen," Keira declared as she sprinkled some spices on the fish.

"I'm hungry; is the food ready yet?" Caleb asked as he reclined on the porch. He took a sip of his beer.

"It'll be done when it's done! Why don't you make yourself useful and see where Zoe and Tristan walked off to?" Keira sounded irritated. She constantly had to remind herself that patience was a virtue whenever she was around her brother. She didn't understand why she reacted the way she did around him, but maybe it was because she'd always had a stronger sense of responsibility than he did. With the way her parents were always busy, if she had relied on Caleb to take care of her, she would have most likely had no food or clean laundry. At a young age, she had already taken on the burden of taking care of her older brother and making sure he didn't destroy the house or skip school. Maybe that's why she was constantly on his case.

Begrudgingly, Caleb walked off onto the trail to see if he'd run into the siblings. "Always so bossy! Can't a guy just catch a break?"

It took Declan a few minutes to realize that he was alone at the cabin with Keira. He didn't know what to say. There was something about Keira that always made Declan feel at home, warm, but at the same time, not at ease. Every time he was alone with her, his heart would start to race, and his mind would go blank.

Keira felt Declan's gaze from behind her and turned toward him. Declan quickly looked away to avoid her gaze. "Deck? Is there something wrong?"

"What? What do you mean?"

"I felt your gaze on my back. Is there something on my shirt?" she asked as she tried to see the back of her shirt.

"No, nothing like that, I was just—"

"Were you checking me out from behind?" Keira taunted with a smirk on her face.

"What? No, I would never ... I mean ... I think you're very attractive, but I wasn't ogling or anything." His face turned tomato red.

Keira broke out in a laugh. "I'm just messing with you. Relax."

Declan relaxed a second and smiled. "You need to stop doing that. You always catch me off guard when you joke around like that."

"Well, you know ... behind every joke there's always a little bit of truth," she said with a small smile.

Declan felt his forehead break into small droplets of sweat. "Um ... I think I'll go help Caleb look for the sibs."

"Why do you do that?" asked Keira looking hurt.

"Do what?" Declan replied turning away from her.

"I mean… we've known each other since the first grade. I care a lot about you, and I think I've made that pretty clear all along. But you always seem to pull away from me. Am I just that undesirable?" She looked down at her feet.

Feeling the pain in Keira's voice, Declan turned back toward her. "I don't pull away from you. I don't know where you're getting this. I could never do that … you … and Caleb are like … family to me."

Keira balled up her hands into fists at her side. "You do pull away from me, Deck, and you know what I'm talking about. Do you really need me to draw you a picture?"

Declan backed away, "Keira, I just…"

"Do you like me, or don't you, Deck? Just tell me now and stop leading me on and pushing me away." Tears welled up in her eyes, threatening to spill out. "It's cruel," she added, tilting her head up to keep the tears from spilling over.

Before Declan could respond, the sliding glass door to the porch opened and Caleb and the Sullivans walked in.

"Okay, found them, and found them hungry! Is food ready yet?" demanded Caleb.

Keira quickly turned back to the grill. "It'll be ready in a few minutes."

"I'll go set the table," said Declan as he walked back into the house.

"You guys looked like you were in a heated conversation; is everything okay?" Caleb whispered as he walked over to Keira.

"We're fine. Can you grab me a few plates? Food's ready," said Keira coldly.

⁎⁎⁎

"I've got to say, I am really impressed with this fish," declared Tristan who was in gastro nirvana and took another bite of his fish. The light crisp of the charred outer surface and soft interior that melted instantly in his mouth made him give off a sound of ecstasy he had never made before. "I've eaten fish cooked by world-renowned chefs, but this makes them taste like dirty rags in comparison."

Keira blushed. "I really can't take credit for this. It's good because it's fresh. The natural flavor of the fish isn't ruined by excessive refrigeration. God made it good."

"You should just take the compliment. He doesn't do that very often," declared Zoe in a serious tone. More sounds of ecstasy filled the dining room as the other two boys took bites of their fillets.

"It's true, Keira; it's so good," Declan added, still avoiding her eyes.

Keira didn't say anything and just looked down at her plate.

Sensing the tension, Caleb said, "Guys, you need to ease off on the compliments, or you'll spoil her and she won't try as hard next time." He then turned to Keira and said, "It's tolerable. Try harder next time."

Keira glared at Caleb. "Well, I wouldn't want to force you to eat something that you'd have to tolerate." She started pulling Caleb's plate away from him.

"Hey, I am a hungry man, and I will eat your hand," declared Caleb pretending that he was about to stab Keira's hand with his fork.

Zoe burst out laughing. "You guys really crack me up."

"You should stick around because every meal is like this. As a matter of fact, it's even more amusing when their parents are around. It's like, 'Caleb, you're such a pig! Keira, don't talk like that to you brother, and act like a lady! At least, I'm not a little midget! Caleb, be nice to your sister! Mom, Caleb licked my fork! Mind your manners young man! Kids, no food fights! Why do you kids insist on acting like ten-year-olds?' For like hours!" Declan mimicked with a large grin on his face.

"It was never that bad...that was way over exaggerated!" exclaimed Caleb, his ears turning bright red.

"Are you saying that such a conversation never happened?" Declan smirked.

"That was like … years ago!"

"You mean like two years ago on your sixteenth birthday?"

"Shut up!" Caleb punched Declan in the arm.

"It must be nice to have so much laughter around the dinner table," said Zoe pensively as the smile slowly faded from her face.

"Oh, I'm so sorry Zoe. I wasn't thinking," replied Declan apologetically.

"Oh, don't worry. I mean, even when my parents were alive, we didn't really interact like that." Zoe looked at her plate blankly as if a flashback was playing out inside her mind.

Everyone was quiet for the next couple minutes as they focused on inhaling their food. Seeing that Zoe's eyes were still watery, Caleb lifted his bottle of beer into the air for an announcement. "To the late Mr. and Mrs. Sullivan, may they rest in peace. Let's remember their lives and the good times you guys had with them." Everyone else raised their glasses and drank.

"Would you like to say something about your mom and dad?" asked Keira, then quickly added, "Only if you feel comfortable about it."

Tristan immediately responded. "I'm definitely not comfortable with this!"

"Wait Tristan, I want to say something," said Zoe as her eyes watered.

"Zoe ...," Tristan warned as he glared at her.

"Please, Tristan. I need this to move on." Zoe continued as a tear streamed down her cheek. "Mom and Dad, you were always strict with us because you wanted to make sure that we were strong. I can't say that I have always understood it, but I think I do now. You weren't always truthful to us, but I believe that you have done that to protect us. You have taught us to protect one another without the help of outsiders. I feel adequately capable and self-sufficient, but I never thought that I would lose you so quickly. I miss you so much, and if there was any way for us to talk to you again—"

"Yes...um...I'm sure Mom and Dad are watching us from up above." Tristan quickly interjected.

Zoe looked up. "Really, where?"

Keira put her hand on top of Zoe's. "They're at home with the Father now. But, they will always be with you in your heart and live on through your memories."

"Let's go for a walk," Tristan suggested to Zoe in a stern tone. He grabbed Zoe by the arm and pulled her away from the dining table.

Keira took a look at Declan. "I'm going for a walk, too. Can you guys manage to clean up?" Apparently, it was a rhetorical question because she got up and left before receiving an answer.

Caleb stood and started gathering the plates. "So … what happened earlier, Deck?"

"What happened? Nothing happened …" Declan replied as he started to help Caleb collect the plates.

"Oh, come on, everyone can tell that you and Keira were in some kind of fight. What were you guys fighting about?" Caleb asked with concern in his voice.

"Nothing, we weren't fighting. I don't know … I can't talk to you about this," declared Declan shaking his head as if trying to clear all the stray thoughts.

"She loves you. I know that, I'm not blind. I mean, ew … gross, my baby sister … but if it has to be someone, I'd rather that person be you. But if you break her heart, I will break your face." He remained silent for a few seconds but then continued. "I know that you like her, too. Your face looks as red as tomato just about every time you see her. Yes, it's that obvious. So… what's the deal?"

"I … do like her … I just can't. I just don't want to talk about this with you." Declan turned his face so that Caleb shouldn't see the conflict that must have been clearly written there.

"Dude, this conversation is embarrassing for me, too! I mean, seeing my baby sister constantly throwing herself at you, it's really more embarrassing for me. So if I'm willing to talk about it … come on, you like her, she likes you, what's the problem?"

"You don't understand," said Declan hesitantly. "I love her, but I can't. If she's with me, all there will be in her future is sorrow. All I can offer her is pain. I can't let that happen to her."

"What are you talking about? Wait, you don't have some weird spanking fetish or something, do you?" Caleb asked jokingly, then screamed "Ah! Stop, T-M-I, T-M-I, don't want to know anymore."

"No! That's not it! What the hell! Can't you stay serious for more than two seconds?" shouted Declan angrily. He got up to leave.

"Wait, wait, sorry. Jokes aside. Why do you think you can only offer her pain? I don't understand you, dude. You seem to always have this dark side of you that you keep from all of us." He caught Declan's shoulder as he tried to walk away.

"You can't understand what it's like because you've never seen it. You've never seen someone whom you love and trust change. Someone who you know loves you and would never hurt you, suddenly turn into someone else who is trying to kill you. In those moments, you look into their eyes, and you see no remnant of the person you love in there. You don't know what that's like, and I hope that you never have to experience it. I've been having nightmares about it almost every night since I was seven." Declan pushed Caleb away and sat down in one of the chairs in the dining room.

"Deck ... I'm sorry about your past. That was a long time ago. Since then, you have us. Your aunt and uncle love you like a son. Are you having trouble trusting or letting others in again?" asked Caleb, having a very real conversation for once in his life.

"No, I love you guys, and I trust you guys. It's me I don't trust!"

"What do you mean?" asked Caleb.

"Mental illness is hereditary. What happened to my mom could very likely happen to me. I don't want Keira to ever have to look into my eyes as I'm trying to kill her. On nights that I don't have a nightmare about my mom, I have nightmares about me suddenly turning on the ones I love and trying to murder them. Do you have any idea what living like that is like? Always being afraid of getting close to someone; afraid to even go to sleep, not knowing what kind of disturbing nightmares might haunt you?"

"Deck … I didn't know … why haven't you ever shared this with us? You know that you can always confide in me. Dude, I'm your best friend," replied Caleb as his eyes started to water up thinking about the pain that his friend was going through.

"Sometimes, I wonder if you guys are even really here. You guys are one of the few good things in my life, maybe too good to be true. I wonder if I had hallucinated, and just imagined that you guys were here, just like how I hallucinate that I can…" Declan stopped, as he couldn't even bring himself to say out loud what he had seen himself do.

"You can't possibly believe that we're just a hallucination. We've known each other for a decade. We've spoken to you and other people at the same time." Caleb placed his hand on Declan's shoulder. "There. Can you feel that? If I was just your imagination, could you have felt that? Deck, we're here for you, no matter what. Don't try to face everything yourself; trust in us. Lean on us."

"Caleb … Of course, I don't really believe that I could have hallucinated all of you, but sometimes I have these thoughts. That's how messed up I am!" Declan rested his head in his hands. "I… I'm sorry about dragging you into my crazy mind. I need some fresh air; I'm going for a walk." Declan stood and walked out into the darkness.

Caleb sat down trying to take in everything that had been revealed to him. He thought about all the great times he had with Declan ever since they were kids. Declan was like the brother that he never had. He'd shared things with Declan that he had never even shared with his sister or his parents. *How could I not have noticed that about my own best friend?*

He thought about all the times that Declan had been there for him. Declan was there to distract him from his broken heart when he broke up with his first girlfriend. He was there to talk him into going back home when he tried to run away in the tenth grade.

Declan always had his back. When he was in sixth grade, the school bully, Joey Thompson harassed him for a whole week. Joey, an eighth grader pushed him against the lockers whenever he passed by and threw paper balls at his head. He finally got fed up and asked Joey if he wanted a piece of him. The eighth grader obliged and took a swing at him. Caleb took a punch to the face and went down. Declan, coming out of nowhere, pounced on Joey and the two of them ended Joey's bullying career. No one respected a bully who was taken down by two sixth graders.

He was always there for me. What kind of best friend am I? All this time, I have allowed him to deal with this all alone.

Then, he suddenly looked up and realized that he was the only one left in the cabin with the dining table full of dishes. "Damn it, why am I always the one left behind to clean up the mess?"

❧⊰⊱☙

Park Ranger Nelly was about to turn in for bed. He had a long day, and he had the early shift again the next day. The state had put sleeping quarters in the ranger's stations. This allowed the park rangers to live in the park, although a more cynical side of him thought that this was a way for the state to put rangers on 24-hour duty without having to pay them for it.

The sleeping quarter was a simple room with a bed, a desk, a chair, and a bathroom. It was a cozy little cabin. Like the rest of the ranger's station, Nelly had brought in many personal touches to make it feel like home. On his desk, Nelly included many pictures of his nephews and nieces. On the floor was a fluffy faux fur rug, and on the walls were a collection of stuffed heads from his many hunts. Nelly had been an excellent hunter when he was younger, and amongst his hunting trophies were the heads of mountain lions, cougars, and bears.

Before turning in for bed, he checked his face in the mirror one last time for any new freckles or moles that might have manifested. To his surprise, he found a few freckles near his temple about midway between his eyes and his ears. Nelly was sure that he had checked that area earlier in the day and didn't see anything. He took a closer look to make sure that there wasn't any strange discoloration. To his horror, it appeared as though half of the freckles were turning red.

Nelly dropped the handheld mirror and ran into his bathroom. He wanted to make sure that he got a clear look at those freckles, so he moved in close to the bathroom mirror and turned on all the lights. Nelly's eyes widened as he saw the freckles grow larger and become blood red. To his horror, they started to bleed.

He quickly took some toilet paper and dabbed at the blood that was trickling down his face. The bleeding intensified, and there was now blood trickling down both sides of this face. His hands started to tremble, and his heart raced as he continued to wipe off the blood. He decided that it was just not working and put pressure on the freckles to stop the bleeding. His heart leaped as his flesh gave way and his fingers sank in when he pushed them onto the freckles. He screamed and ran out of his bathroom. Running too quickly, he tripped on the rug and fell.

He looked down at his hands again, and the blood that he saw before was gone. He heard a low growl behind him and as he turned around to look, a large mountain lion stared him in the face. He jumped backward as he shrieked, only to hit something large and soft behind him. He turned around to look, and all he saw were teeth.

CHAPTER 15
-TRISTAN AND ZOE-

"**W**hat is happening to you? You're not yourself. The Zoe I know would never show weakness in front of a few puny humans," Tristan declared as he walked up to Zoe, who had her back towards him. The moon was so bright, it reflected from the surface of Lake Louisa outlining Zoe's silhouette. The sounds of crickets echoed through the night, and Tristan cringed at the sounds. Tristan hated crickets ever since he encountered his first demon at the age of eleven. His parents had brought back the remains of a possession victim. Before his parents were able to properly lock up the jar with the remains, Tristan came into contact with it. The demon, as revenge to the elder Sullivans for his entrapment, gave Tristan the most horrific hallucination. Tristan saw himself running in the fields when the ground below him opened up. He fell into a hive of crickets. There were thousands of crickets all around him, and he started to drown in the swarm of them. They started to enter his nose, mouth, and ears. There were so many crickets that piled on top of him that his vision was blurred, and all he could hear were deafening sounds of cricket chirping.

"You sound just like them, you know?" said Zoe.

"Like who?" asked Tristan as his skin started to crawl.

"Like Mom and Dad. Or whoever they were. We were raised to see ourselves different from humans. To have a certain level of disdain towards them, even. They've already lied to us about who they were; how do we know that they haven't lied to us about who we are? Or what we are? What if we are no different from the 'humans' we were brought up to despise?"

"No different? I could have squashed them all like flies back there. Except for the girl, I'd keep her," said Tristan with a smirk on his face.

"Stop it, Tristan. You're sounding like a demon. We were raised to set ourselves apart from them, and maybe even despise them, but we were never taught to oppress or conquer them," said Zoe staring into the moon's reflection on the lake.

"Are you kidding me? Think of how we treated our servants at home. We were raised to rule over them," declared Tristan as he scanned around for the annoying chirping crickets.

"Well, I don't see it that way anymore. I'm tired of feeling different from everyone else. It's lonely. I just want to be a part of something. Have friends. Joke around like Caleb and Keira." Zoe smiled as she thought about her time with them.

"We'll never be able to be like 'them.' Can you imagine what it would be like if the 'humans' find out what we can do? They would look at us like monsters; like... demons. They would have us locked away or experimented on. They will try anyway," Tristan added in a tone that sounded like a threat.

"I don't think that Caleb and the others are like that," declared Zoe indignantly.

"Humans are all like that. Your actions affect me, too, Zoe. This was a mistake. We should have never come here with them. We should leave now. I forbid you to talk to them again," Tristan demanded as he turned her to face him.

"No," Zoe stated calmly.

"What do you mean, no?" Tristan demanded furiously as he grabbed Zoe's wrist tightly.

"I plan on staying for the rest of the trip and to be friends with Caleb. I will see who I want to see and do what I want to do. And there's nothing you can do about it! Now let go of my wrist!" demanded Zoe staring Tristan right in the eyes.

"No! And if I catch you talking to those … humans again, I will-" growled Tristan as his grip tightened.

"I said, let go!" yelled Zoe. Tristan felt his hand lose control as his grip was pried apart by an invisible force.

Rage flared up within him and before he could control himself, he slapped Zoe in the face as he said, "You dare to use your powers against me!" The rage on his face faded and a look of shock remained. He had never raised his hands to his sister before.

Zoe held her face with her hand with the same look of shock on it as was on her brother's.

"Zoe … I … I'm sorry … the crickets … they …" stammered Tristan feeling guilty.

As tears streamed down Zoe's face, she whispered, "Stay away from me," and she ran off in a blur.

Tristan wanted to chase after Zoe, but his body wouldn't respond to his desire to follow her. He knew that it was pointless now. She needed time to cool off. He couldn't believe that he would hit his sister. They had argued in the past, but they had never fought physically or used their abilities against each other. Now that their parents were gone, Zoe was all that he had left.

It was the crickets' fault. They irritated me so much. I didn't know what I was doing.

He noticed that the chirping had stopped. The sound of the slap was so loud that it scared the crickets away.

Tristan sat down dejectedly on the pier and stared into the lake at the reflection of the moon. He thought about the times when they were younger and their parents were training them how to fight. They would always fight either their mother or father, but never against each other.

He remembered six months ago when they had tracked a demon-possessed man back to a vampire hive. They had fought off twenty vampires alone. Just as they were about to escape, one of the vampires shot him. The bullet pierced his lungs, which were quickly filled with his blood, making it hard for him to breath. Zoe picked him up and continued running until they were safe. For the next couple of days, she had nursed him back to health.

Zoe had his back that time, and always. And, if he ever got injured during a fight, she was always there to take care of him. He hated himself for letting his anger take hold of him.

Damn crickets!

He sat there for a while pondering how he was going to patch things up with Zoe. Suddenly, he heard the crunching of footsteps behind him. He quickly turned around and saw Keira. Keira didn't say anything, but just walked up to him and sat down. He had wanted to sulk alone, but oddly when she sat down next to him, he felt a sense of calming comfort. He'd never really had that feeling before; therefore, he remained silent.

Keira broke the silence. "Isn't it just so calming to watch the reflection of the moon and listen to the sounds of the rolling waves. Whenever I sit here, I feel all my troubles just washing away."

"I guess," replied Tristan, unsure of what he was feeling. All he knew was that he felt peace for the first time, and it felt strange.

"So... what happened?" asked Keira as her usual gentle demeanor dropped, and she glared at Tristan.

"What do you mean, 'what happened?'" asked Tristan suspiciously.

"I heard a sound like a large crack and heard you apologizing to Zoe. When I got close enough to see you, Zoe wasn't anywhere to be seen. So... what happened?" Keira insisted.

"Nothing, we just had a disagreement," replied Tristan feeling relieved that she hadn't heard their conversation.

"Is that how you guys normally settle matters at home? I mean, that slap was quite loud. I was so far away that I couldn't even make out your shape, but I heard that slap. Do you find it acceptable to hit women?" asked Keira in a harsh tone giving him a stern look.

"No, of course not! I … I don't know what came over me. I've been beating myself up about it ever since," stammered Tristan looking down. *Why am I explaining myself? Why do I even care what she thinks?*

"Good, I wouldn't have approached you if I thought you were one of those violent men who wouldn't think twice about hitting women. So, you feel bad about it. What are you going to do to make it up to her?" asked Keira insistently.

"I don't know. I said I was sorry. What do you want me to do, buy her a gift or something?" muttered Tristan turning to stare at her.

"No, you dolt! Go find her. Let her know what she means to you, and let her know that you will never do it again. Now go! What are you waiting for?" Keira stood up and grabbed Tristan by the collar of his shirt and hauled him to his feet.

Who in the world does this chick thinks she is? Tristan stared at her blankly. "You know, you're quite bold. You approached a guy who might or might not have a problem with violence alone in a dark wooded area. In addition to that, you're making demands of him. You're really something else."

Keira blushed a little, but luckily, it wasn't visible to Tristan since it was so dark.

"I wouldn't stand so close to him if I were you," said a voice from behind them. Keira turned around and saw Park Ranger Nelly.

"Oh, hey Nelly. You really startled me. Is there a problem?" asked Keira confused by the presence of Nelly.

"Yes, I have some matters to settle with your friend," demanded Nelly as he slowly approached them.

"Oh? Do you know Tristan?" asked Keira as Nelly's face became clearer in the moonlight as he approached. His face startled Keira. His face was ghastly white, and there were dark circles around his sunken eyes. "Are you okay? You don't look so well," asked Keira sounding concerned.

Nelly was now standing directly in front of Keira. He grabbed her by the shoulder and threw her to his right as he yelled, "Get out of my way, bitch!" Keira flew through the air screaming.

Tristan had sensed something strange about him but was caught off guard with Nelly's attack. He immediately ran to Nelly's right to catch Keira as she flew through the air. They both landed softly about twenty feet away from Nelly. Tristan moved in front of Keira and said, "Run!" *Why am I protecting her? Why do I even care what happens to this ... human?*

Keira backed off a few feet but didn't run away. "Nelly, what happened to you? What is going on?" Fear turned into confusion as she realized how far Nelly had flung her.

Nelly blurred as he ran toward Tristan. The two started fighting, and the punches and kicks were flying around so quickly that Keira could barely follow what was happening. She had never seen anything so frightening, but yet so amazing, before. The two moved at extraordinary speeds, but Tristan's movements were so graceful and precise that it was almost beautiful.

From behind her, Keira heard Declan's voice. "Keira!" She turned around and saw Declan running toward her. "Keira, are you okay? I heard your scream so I started running in your direction. What's happening? Why are Tristan and Nelly fighting?" asked Declan with concern and confusion.

"I don't know Deck, Nelly ... he doesn't seem to be himself," replied Keira, still bewildered by the movements of the two.

Nelly and Tristan started moving quicker, and it seemed to be a blur to Keira. "I can't really see what's going on anymore ... They're moving so fast. How is this possible?"

Declan was confused by the question. He saw the two fighting perfectly clearly. "I'm not sure what you mean, but it seems that Nelly means business. Every blow he's struck toward Tristan was aimed at his vitals. They're not just fighting; Nelly's trying to kill Tristan!"

"I will kill you this time. That girl isn't here to help you. You are an unwanted breed that needs to be snuffed out," hissed Nelly as he continued to attack Tristan.

"Vetis! I thought you didn't do the whole possession thing? You're not going to get away that easily this time. So what happened? You're so much slower this time," Tristan chided.

"That comes with the territory of a new host, but it's more than enough to take care of a brat like you," yelled Nelly as he blurred toward Tristan.

Just before Nelly reached Tristan, Declan grabbed hold of Nelly and tried to restrain him on the ground.

"Nelly, what has gotten into you? What is going on?" asked Declan as he wrestled Nelly down.

"You! You're the boy from the other night! How is it possible? You're another—" demanded Nelly,

"We have to get him into the lake. Running water washes away his powers," Tristan interrupted as he helped Declan restrain Nelly to the ground.

"What?" asked Declan, assuming that he must have misheard.

Without hesitating, Tristan dragged both Declan and Nelly into the lake. Tristan pushed Nelly's face into the water.

"What the hell are you doing?" Declan yelled, confused and startled at what Tristan was doing.

"If he's not fully submerged, he will escape again," declared Tristan as he continued to force Nelly's head below the water surface.

"Stop it! You're going to kill him!" demanded Declan, grabbing at Tristan's hand to try and stop his violence. Tristan strained against Declan's hand, but could not push Nelly's face further into the water and was slowly being pulled up by Declan. He realized that he wouldn't be able to overpower Declan. He released Nelly's head and jumped away from Declan.

"How are you … it's not impossible … you're one of them," said Tristan, accusingly, with confusion on his face.

Declan ignored Tristan. He realized Nelly had stopped breathing. Pulling Nelly out of the water, he started giving Nelly CPR. Nelly spat out some water and started breathing again but wasn't able to stay conscious.

"Call 911," Declan yelled to the startled Keira.

∞∞

Caleb came running up to Declan and Keira as they were carrying an unconscious Nelly toward the main road. "Hey, what's going on? I can hear the sound of the ambulance coming up the road. Why is the ranger unconscious?"

Keira ran up to her brother and hugged him tightly. "It was horrible, Caleb. Nelly completely lost it and started attacking us. He didn't seem like himself at all. He seemed like a completely different person. And the way he looked … his eyes …" Keira shuttered and couldn't continue.

"It's okay, Keira. It's going to be okay. Are you hurt anywhere?" asked Caleb as he examined Keira.

"No, it was as if Nelly was trying to kill Tristan," cried Keira with a shaky voice.

"Where are Tristan and Zoe?"

Declan looked around, confused. "I haven't seen Zoe, but Tristan was just here," The arrival of the ambulance broke up the conversation.

Caleb motioned toward the EMTs. "You go tell the EMTs what they need to know. We'll go to find the Sullivans."

Declan gave a brief summary to the EMTs. "Hi, I'm Declan Peters. I'm a UAP at the Central Florida Behavioral Center. This man's mental capacity is unstable. He stopped breathing for about a minute and was resuscitated. We need to take him to the center. We have the equipment and personnel there to treat both his physical and psychological conditions. Can I tag along?" Declan hopped onto the ambulance alongside the EMTs and it took off towards the center.

ഔഇൔ

Declan rushed through the emergency doors of his work place along with the EMTs who were pushing Nelly on a gurney.

"We have a male patient who is still unconscious after resuscitation from drowning. Possible brain damage; patient was mentally unstable prior to losing unconsciousness and therefore should be restrained," shouted one of the EMTs.

"Declan, what's going on? What happened?" asked Joe, after noticing the commotion in the hallway. He'd never seen Declan looking so serious.

"I'm not sure. We were out at Lake Louisa. The park ranger just lost it and started attacking us," Declan explained as he tried to settle his nerves.

Joe helped the other medical personnel transfer Nelly onto a hospital bed. "Don't worry, Declan. We'll take good care of him. You should probably sit this one out. I can restrain him." Joe started putting restraints on the unconscious park ranger.

Joe was worried that this might be hitting too close to home for Declan as the situation was similar to his mother's. Declan understood Joe's concern and nodded at him.

"Okay, but I'll be outside in the waiting room. Please let me know how he is as soon as he wakes," Declan said with a trembling voice.

CHAPTER 16
-TRISTAN-

Tristan walked into his hotel room, crestfallen. He didn't even turn on the lights as he continued into his room and laid on his back. The events of the night ran through his head. He thoroughly examined each event. *Declan was somehow fast enough to get between Vetis and I. One reason would be that Declan was himself also possessed. But why would they fight each other? No, that can't possibly be right. Declan had also practically overpowered me while I was trying to drown that park ranger. If Declan had been possessed, the running water underneath him would have washed away his strength just like Vetis. The only logical explanation was that Declan was like Zoe and me ... whatever we are.*

Tristan sat up from his bed and turned to the nightstand. He opened up the drawer and pulled out a picture frame that he had thrown into the drawer the other day out of anger. He turned the frame right side up, and it revealed an image of his parents. His eyes burned as tears built up.

"You told us that we were one of a kind... that we were special... that we were the descendants of the angels," Tristan said softly to the picture. "You lied to me. I hate you."

He looked up and around the room. "If you're here and you can hear me, I HATE YOU!"

Suddenly, there was a knock on his hotel room door. Tristan stayed quiet and waited. There was a knock again.

"Mr. Sullivan, please open up. We're the FBI, we have some questions for you," said the voice from outside the room.

The FBI! Tristan thought. *It must be the humans. They have reported my abilities to the authorities, and now they've come to experiment on me. They want me? Let's see how many of them are willing to sacrifice to have me.*

Tristan confidently walked to the door and opened it wide. "You want a piece of me ..."

Tristan didn't finish his comment when he realized there were only two men in suits outside his room, and they didn't have any weapons drawn.

The two suited agents looked at each other before one of them said, "Um... Mr. Sullivan, did we catch you at a bad time?"

"Yes! What do you want?" asked Tristan now back into his normal unreadable demeanor.

"This is Agent Warren and I'm Agent Peterson. We're from the FBI. Can we have a chat with you?"

"That point is moot, you're already talking," said Tristan, irritated by their presence.

"We've been meaning to have a chat with you all day. We gave instructions to the hotel to inform us when you returned." Agent Warren hid his annoyance of being mouthed off by a teenager.

"Okay ... it is rather late in the night," said Tristan with a mild agitation in his voice.

"It's regarding the death of your parents," said Agent Warren, satisfied when he saw a crack in Tristan's stone-faced demeanor.

This caught Tristan's attention. *It would be a lot easier for me to kill them if they were inside and out of the hallway.*

"Please excuse the way I reacted earlier, as you can imagine what I'm currently feeling," he said as he invited the two agents into his room. He guided them to sit down at the dining table.

"I apologize for doing this to you, but I need to show you something." Agent Peterson pulled out two photos. Tristan recognized one of the photos at once; it was an image that was stuck in his head for the past couple of days.

"Why are you showing me a picture of my parent's remains?" demanded Tristan with a little anger in his voice.

"According to the statement by the coroner, these two photos were taken within six hours of each other," explained Agent Warren.

Tristan peered at the photos more closely. One of the photos contained two people, lying side by side, their skin tinged a slight blue. The other one was disturbing. It showed two people but here, they were skeletal, their bones brown and with slight patches of skin hanging from portions of bone, the jaws wide open as if in a scream.

"This level of rapid deterioration doesn't typically happen," Agent Warren continued.

Tristan stiffened but thought that he hid it well since the two agents didn't react. "Okay, so ... ask some forensics guy to figure it out. Why are you coming to me about this? As a matter of fact, I ought to sue the city for negligence on the handling of my parent's remains," stated Tristan, trying to sound irritated to mask his nervousness on the subject.

"We don't think that it was negligence on the coroner's part that has caused this because we've seen this kind of deterioration before.

Tristan readied his body to pounce onto the two agents.

I will first punch Agent Warren in the neck to break his trachea, and then I'll jump onto the table and kick Agent Peterson on the side of the face, breaking his neck.

Agent Peterson pulled out another photo. "Have you ever seen this man before?"

Tristan hesitated for a moment. He wasn't ready for that. He had assumed that somehow they had associated his parent's irregular remains with demons. He looked at the photo closely. "It looks like some strangely buff old guy. Never seen him before."

Looking disappointed, Agent Peterson put the photo away. "I'm sorry we have bothered you then."

The two agents started to rise. "Wait one second," demanded Tristan. "You come into my hotel room and force me to look at disturbing pictures of my parents' dead bodies, then throw out some picture of an old guy who might or might not be a suspect. Do you expect to leave it just like that? I want some answers!"

The two agents looked at each other. Agent Warren spoke up. "We've been tracking a series of unexplained rapid deterioration of body remains in the southeast for about three years now. We think it's probably been happening since way before that, but we've only been on this case for the past three years. And for more than a few of these cases, we've found surveillance camera footage of this man lurking around the crime scenes at the initial estimated time of death."

"Do you think that this man is somehow linked to all these deaths?"

"We're not sure how he's causing it, but it appears that he's somehow linked to it," answered Agent Peterson, as he received a glare from Agent Warren.

"How would one go about causing bodies to deteriorate rapidly like that?" asked Tristan innocently, trying to see where the authorities were going with it.

"We're thinking that he might be testing some sort of bio-weapon that would kill the victim but leaves the remains looking aged. But we had our forensics team examine the remains closely to see if any bacteria or virus was present, and they found nothing. The point is, we're not really sure how he's doing it, but we're here to find out."

"So do you know who this guy is? How are you going about locating him?" asked Tristan with true excitement in his voice.

"We haven't been able to identify him yet. We ran all our facial recognition programs. This guy doesn't seem to have any ID, driver's license, or criminal record," Agent Peterson said.

"We've already said too much," said Agent Warren abruptly as he gave Agent Peterson a glance. Both agents stood up.

Maybe you guys have used all your resources to find him, but I have my own ways.

CHAPTER 17
-DECLAN-

Declan stayed in the waiting room for about an hour. There wasn't anything else for him to do but wait. He figured he might as well pay a visit to his mother while he was there. He felt nervous as he walked toward her room, which was now on the fifth floor after her sudden meltdown the other day.

Will she be normal again when I walk through the door? Or will she try to attack me?

He remembered the look on Nelly's face as he attacked Tristan. He had seen that look before; it was the same look that his mother had on her face every time she attacked him. That same grimace and menacing eyes had haunted him in his nightmares for years.

Come to think of it, I saw that look recently. That new patient they admitted the other day, Kyle. Will I have that look on my face when I finally snap?

He pictured himself with that same grimace, dark circles under his eyes and the dilated pupils. He shuddered.

Declan was lost in his thoughts as he arrived on the fifth floor. As he opened the door from the stairs, the hallway lay in front of him. It was a long hall with many locked rooms. The room doors had large windows that allowed the medical personnel to look through safely without having to open the door. The rooms were all painted white and were padded so that the patients inside couldn't hurt themselves. Other rooms on the floor without the padded walls and floors had no furniture other than a bed, which had heavy leather restraints. The patients in non-padded rooms were heavily sedated and restrained to their bed as the medication worked through their bodies.

Unconsciously, Declan's hand searched for the pendant around his neck once again as he approached his mother's room. Panic ran through his entire body as his hand made contact with his bare neck. Frantically, both his hands searched around his neck area, but the pendant was nowhere to be found. His heart pounded, and an empty feeling stabbed at it as he thought of never seeing the pendant again.

As he searched, he passed by one of the doors with the large windows. He tried to use the reflection on the window to see if he could see the pendant. Through the window, he saw his new coworker, Victor, inside the room. Declan was amazed that Victor was already working on the fifth floor considering he was new. The center had strict protocols for training to reach the different floors regardless of experience.

Declan was curious as he pressed his face against the window to get a closer look at what was going on. He saw that the patient who resided in that room was Kyle, and he was restrained to his bed.

Well, that's good, considering how unstable he was the other day.

The two seemed to be having a heated conversation. Declan could tell that there was anger in Kyle's face, but couldn't see Victor's face since his back was toward the window. He saw Victor lift something up and press it down onto Kyle's forearm; Kyle screamed in pain. Declan was furious. He had heard stories about medical personnel who abused patients to satisfy their own sick pleasures. He'd seen reports about patients who were found with wounds like cigarette burns or cuts. The medical personnel would claim the wounds were self-inflicted.

Declan burst through the door. "What do you think you're doing? Get away from him!"

Victor immediately turned toward Declan. "Declan? You don't understand. I'm trying to help him."

"You're a sicko!" demanded Declan as he rushed toward Victor and pushed him away from Kyle. Declan had pushed Victor so hard that Victor smacked against the opposite wall with a loud crack as the wall behind the padding split.

"I will make sure that you never work here a..." Declan couldn't finish his statement as Kyle broke through the restraints and put Declan into a headlock from behind. "What are you doing, Kyle? I'm trying to save you from this guy," choked Declan. All he could hear was Kyle cackling as everything around him started to darken. The last thing Declan saw was Victor pulling out a Taser gun when all of a sudden his entire body jolted with pain.

ಬಿಞಛಿ

Declan was awakened by the sounds of screams. As vision slowly returned, he could see that he was sitting in an empty room. His hands were bound by some kind of chain behind him and his legs were bound to the legs of a chair. Above him hung a light bulb that supplied all the light in the room. Declan's heart leaped as another sudden scream came from the adjacent room. His heart continued to race as he looked around to take in the surroundings. He didn't know what to think. The last thing he remembered was rushing into Kyle's padded room. The images of Victor abusing Kyle came back, and finally, the image of Victor pulling out a Taser gun returned to him.

What to do? What to do? Oh, my god, I've been kidnapped!

His eyes frantically searched for an exit. He saw that there was a door directly across the room from him. In front of the door, lying on the floor was something that looked like a beaded necklace. He concentrated his gaze to see if it was something that he could possible use. All of a sudden, the necklace floated up into the air. Declan squeezed his eyes shut and shook his head.

Damn it! Not the time to hallucinate!

He opened up his eyes and saw the necklace on the floor again.

Did the necklace look like it had moved from its original position? He shook his head again. *The damn necklace isn't going to help me after all! How did I get here? Who did this to me? Victor? What if it's some kind of serial killer? What to do? What to do?*

Declan took a deep breath.

Pull yourself together!

He took several more deep breaths.

All I need to do is to free myself from these constraints, get out, and call the police.

He felt around the chains that were around his wrists. Strangely, the chains didn't really feel like just chains. They were more like beads.

Could it be that the necklace on the floor is the same material that he used to restrain me?

With a little effort, Declan pulled his wrists away from each other and the beaded chain shattered easily. Declan felt down to his legs. Once again, he felt the same beaded chains. He gave the chain a light tug and the beads fell down to the floor.

This guy is not the sharpest tool in the shed.

Declan got up and wobbled. His muscles were still slightly numb from the jolt of electricity that Victor had used to put him down. Slowly, he got to the door of the room, and he turned the knob.

Wow...this is a whole new level of stupid. They didn't even lock the door.

He opened the door to see a hallway, and at the end of the hallway, there was a staircase that led downward. Across the room, he noticed a window. Declan peeked outside and found that he was in a residential neighborhood.

I'm in a two-story house.

He slowly crept toward the staircase. The wooden floors under his feet creaked as he tiptoed down the hall. Every sound from the old floors made Declan's heart jump and the hairs on the back of his neck stand. As he passed by the adjacent room where the screams came from earlier, more screams erupted. Declan wanted to ignore the screams and run, but he couldn't. He pressed his ear up to the door to hear what was going on.

"Do you wish to be saved? You must want this for yourself for it to work. If you are not fully committed to asking the Lord to remove this demon, it won't happen. Do you understand?" Declan recognized it as Victor's voice.

"Yes, please help me," replied a trembling voice.

Images of Declan's mother came flooding back into his mind. "I will get you demon! I will kill you if it's the last thing I do!" Then it became clear to Declan. Victor must have finally lost it after working in the industry for so many years.

"When all you do is see crazy people every day, eventually some of it rubs off on you," Joe had told Declan once when Declan had asked him why he took a sabbatical every four years.

Declan pressed his ear back toward the door and heard, "I cast you out Bifrons in the name of..." yelled Victor, but his voice got covered with the most horrifying scream of agony.

Declan couldn't stand by the door listening anymore. He grabbed the lamp next to him and kicked open the door. What he saw then would give Declan nightmares for many years to come. Kyle was bound to a chair as Declan had been, but his face was so ghastly white that it looked blue. His eyes had such menace that Declan's heart pounded as he looked into them. Kyle had a grimace of agony on his face, and his mouth had opened at least three to four times larger than humanly possible.

Victor held a crucifix in one hand and a small metallic tube in the other. A writhing dark shape climbed out of Kyle's mouth. As the shape moved, Declan saw that it looked up directly at him with red glowing eyes. Declan jumped as he saw the dark shape, and the hairs on the back of his neck stood.

"No!" screamed Victor as the door swung opened and the writhing shape swarmed toward Declan. Declan didn't know what to do so he crossed his arms in front of him to shield his face. The dark entity slammed against Declan, pushing him backward, and slammed him into the wall. As the entity made contact with Declan, he noticed a strange red glow that seemed to have encompassed his forearms. The entity then moved down the stairs and disappeared into the shadows.

"It escaped! Damn it!" Victor spat. He ran to the small side table in the corner of the room, grabbed the flask that was on it, and ran toward Declan. He emptied the flask onto Declan and pressed his crucifix onto Declan's forehead. Declan squeezed his eyes shut and shook his head in disbelief of what he had just seen, but then he realized what was being done to him.

"Get off of me, you sick bastard!" demanded Declan. Victor looked stunned and backed away from Declan. "What the hell was that?"

"You're ... not possessed," stammered Victor sounding confused.

Declan swung the lamp he had in his hand at Victor. Victor recovered quickly from his shock and jumped back in time to dodge the swing. Declan stood up and held the lamp in an offensive stance.

"Declan, you need to calm down," said Victor in a reassuring voice.

Declan noticed that the lamp he held in his hand was shaking, and realized that his entire body was shaking. Declan tried to steady his body when the sounds of soft sobbing came from Kyle. Declan slammed the lamp against the wall behind him, and the bulb at the top of the lamp shattered.

Pointing the jagged glass end of the lamp toward Victor he yelled, "Stay back! You, psycho!" He carefully walked around to Kyle, never letting his eyes leave Victor, keeping the lamp pointed at him.

"Hey, Kyle, are you okay? Don't worry. I won't let him hurt you anymore. I'm going to get you out of here," Declan said trying to reassure Kyle.

"It's gone," Kyle said, sobbing, relieved.

"What did you say?" asked Declan not letting his eyes move from Victor.

"I'm finally free from it. Oh, thank God!" declared Kyle as his soft sobs broke into a loud cry.

"Declan, no one here is sick. What you just witnessed was an exorcism," declared Victor with finality in his voice.

"Do you even hear yourself, man? Exorcism? You've lost it!" said Declan still pointing the lamp at him.

"Well, if I'm the one who's sick, what threw you against the wall?"

The image of the dark shape that had darted toward him filled Declan's mind, and he shuddered. "I'm not sure ... I must have just fallen backward," stammered Declan, not wanting to believe what had just happened. *That was real? It wasn't my imagination or a hallucination?*

Declan looked at Kyle and saw that there was color in Kyle's face now, and the sullen sunken eyes were now gone. Kyle's eyes now looked relieved and gentle. "This can't be true ..." Declan continued. "Maybe, I really am losing it." Declan felt his legs give in and he fell to the floor.

"Well, considering you just witnessed the most horrifying part of an exorcism, I think that you're doing relatively well," Victor stated as he walked toward Declan. He reached his hand down to Declan, but Declan backed up and pointed the lamp at Victor again.

"Declan, you have nothing to fear from me. As you saw, I was helping Kyle. Look at him. Doesn't he look much better than before?" Victor asked softly, his eyes wide and sincere.

Declan looked over and confirmed Victor's words. "But ... what ..." stammered Declan not quite able to get the words out.

"Come on, drop the lamp and get up. Let's go get some food for Kyle. I don't think he's eaten in days," said Victor as he slowly reached for the jagged lamp that was pointed at him and moved it out of the way.

Victor held his hand out to Declan and hauled him up. He then turned to Kyle. "You'll be safe in this room. This room is blessed, and it won't be able to enter. So, just relax and rest up. I'll return soon with something for you to eat and a bed for you to rest on."

Declan followed Victor down the stairs and into the kitchen. Victor took out two cans of chicken noodle soup from one of the cupboards and started to warm the soup on the stove.

"So … where are we right now?" asked Declan as he looked around trying to find a window to look through.

"This was one of many safe houses set up around the world. We exorcists reside in these safe houses while we're on the job," replied Victor, not looking up as he continued working on the meal for Kyle.

"Right … exorcists around the world … you make it sound like some secret society or some conspiracy that's been hidden from us or something," replied Declan mockingly.

"No, there's no conspiracy. The type of work we do has been published all around the world, just read your Bible. The safe houses aren't used to keep our secret from you, but from the demons."

"Look, I'm still not sure what I just saw…"

"Kyle was possessed by a demon. The demon tried to take control of him. It tried to force him into submission through starvation and all kinds of other methods of torture. What you witnessed was me exorcising the demon from his body. And I emphasize the fact that this *was* a safe house before your interference allowed the demon to escape and compromise this location." Victor scowled as he looked up and glared at Declan.

"What do you mean I allowed it to escape?" asked Declan defensively.

"Well, I had blessed the room and holy water was sprinkled on every wall and on the door. Once I exorcised the demon, it would have nowhere to go, and I would have bound it in a vial to be locked up. When you kicked down the door, you created an opening for the demon to escape." Victor explained in a slow and articulate manner as if explaining something fundamental to a young child.

Declan was dumbstruck. "How can you blame me for that? You're the one who kidnapped me without telling me anything. You can't blame me for wanting to help Kyle. Besides, your idea of restraining people sucks. I mean who ties people up with beaded necklaces anyway? You didn't even lock my room door."

"Those were not just beaded bracelets; those were rosaries. I had assumed that you were also possessed by your display of strength back at the hospital. The rosary would have held you down. And I can blame you because you're the one who opened the door wide for a demon to pass through," replied Victor in the same patronizing tone while focusing on the pot of soup once again.

"Well, why didn't you bless all the walls of this house? Wouldn't the demon have been stuck on his way out if you did?" asked Declan defiantly.

"I didn't account for the possibility of someone who I thought was possessed to break through the rosaries. Nor did I anticipate that you would be able to exit through a blessed room and break into mine. So now the demon will torment another person and come back for revenge."

"I... I thought that you told Kyle he'd be safe here," said Declan nervously.

"For a while, it will be safe. Until the demon finds a new host, it will not be able to interact with the physical world. My turn to ask some questions! How was it possible for the demon to physically push you backward in its spirit form? It shouldn't be able to interact with you. It should have either gone through you or entered you. And how do you explain your inhuman strength?" Victor looked up from the pot at Declan with suspicion in his eyes.

"Adrenaline! Have you never heard of that? I'm sure they identified that even when you were in school," demanded Declan in a tone of mockery and defiance. Then suddenly, Declan snapped his head back for a second in a moment of understanding, "Wait a minute! You thought I was possessed? Was that why you dumped water on me and pressed a crucifix on me?"

"Yes, the holy water and crucifix would have immobilized you with agony while I dragged you into the room to perform the exorcism on you," said Victor.

"How would some water and a cross immobilize me? What is this some corny vampire movie?" mocked Declan.

"Holy water is water that has been imbued with the holiness of God, and the cross is, of course, a reminder of who the Lord Jesus Christ is. Upon contact with either of these items, the demon is reminded of the holiness of the Living God and all the wrong they have done come back to the forefront. The guilt that the demon senses is completely unbearable for them. Now, stop trying to avoid my questions by being a smart ass," replied Victor sternly.

"I … I don't know. Sometimes I just feel this energy inside of me. I don't know how, and I don't even think about it; it just happens. I have always assumed that I was hallucinating. I have always been afraid that they were signs that I was starting to lose my mind … like my mother," replied Declan with the last part coming out as a whisper.

Victor picked up the pot and poured out its contents into a bowl. He placed a spoon into the bowl and placed it onto a tray with a few dinner rolls on it. He got up and started walking back up the stairs. He noticed that Declan had remained seated at the kitchen counter. "Declan, can you please help me bring up that futon mattress by the couch?" Declan grabbed the mattress and followed Victor into Kyle's room. When they entered, they saw that Kyle had backed himself into the corner of the room, hugging his knees to his chest. His face was still wet with tears, but he appeared to be calmer now.

"Here Kyle, have some soup. We'll set up a futon here for you to sleep on. Eat up, have a good sleep, and we'll talk in the morning," Victor said. With that, he placed the tray of soup and dinner rolls down on the floor next to Kyle. He took the futon mattress from Declan and placed it on the floor. Victor signaled to Declan to leave with him,

"Are you sure we should just leave him alone?" asked Declan as he stared at the disoriented Kyle. Kyle slowly reached for the spoon and as he picked it up, his hands shook. Kyle used his other hand to steady the shaky spoon to attempt to eat the soup.

"He's going to need some time on his own to sort things out. When someone is possessed by a demon, it causes a level of spiritual damage. When the Lord made man, He gave us free will, and when that free will is compromised, it leaves a trauma that will take time to heal. Not only does a demon try to take its victim's will away, it constantly shows its host all kinds of demented hallucinations to try to trick them into giving in. Some victims spend years trying to decipher what's reality and what are hallucinations given by the demon." Victor led Declan back down the stairs.

"So… what's going to happen to him? Are you going to send him back to the center to recover from the … trauma?" asked Declan as he followed Victor.

"No, we actually have a facility specifically made for recovering victims. He'll spend however long he needs there to rehabilitate himself, and he'll need physical therapy. That demon must have dislocated most of the joints in his body at one time or another." Victor sat down on the couch in the living room. He gestured to Declan to sit while Declan cringed at the comment.

The living room was simple with a loveseat, sofa, and coffee table. The walls were painted white and bare. Other than the food that was in the kitchen, the place looked like a vacant furnished rental property.

"Won't people ask questions when they discover that he is missing from the center?"

"No, I've already had his parents fill out transfer papers yesterday morning when I decided that I would perform the exorcism. His parents were actually the ones who sought my help. Once I confirmed Kyle's situation, I explained it all to his parents, and they agreed to let me help. Now if you're done with your questions, let's talk about your abilities again. What do you mean when you say you feel a power inside of you? And why would you think that you were losing your mind?" Victor stared at Declan as if analyzing him.

Declan took a deep breath and sighed. "My … my mother is a patient at the center. She's been there since I was seven. Since mental illness is hereditary, I think one day I might end up like her. So, whenever I think I've done or seen something that seemed extraordinary, I would force myself to believe that I had imagined or hallucinated it."

"Well, it seemed pretty real to me. When you threw me against the wall at the center, it could have fooled me that you were demon possessed. I've never seen such strength and speed other than from the possessed." Victor rubbed the bruise on the back of his neck as he winced.

"Could it be that there's a demon inside of me? Whenever my mother had a meltdown, she would call me a demon child and try to drown me," Declan said with real fear in his eyes.

"No, it's not possible. If you were possessed, you would not have been able to break the rosaries tying you down. And the holy water and crucifix have had some kind of affect on you." Victor replied confidently, but there was something in Victor's eyes that told Declan that he was holding something back.

"What? What is it that you're not telling me?" demanded Declan impatiently.

"Well, it might be nothing, but I just find it interesting that she tried to drown you," replied Victor as his eyes brightened.

Anger welled up inside Declan. "Interesting? You find it 'interesting' that a mother tries to drown her own seven-year-old? You find it 'interesting' that a kid had to watch his own mother try to snuff out his life?" Declan stood up with his hands balled up in a tight fist.

"I'm sorry, Declan. It came out all wrong. It's just that, if you were demon possessed, then the method of choice for a hunter would be drowning. I find it … strange … that your mother, in her state of dementia, would stumble upon a feasible method of dealing with demonic possession." Victor held his hands up in a gesture of apology.

Declan's shoulders and fists relaxed. "A hunter? Like a demon hunter? Is that what you are? Is that what you do … hunt demons?"

"No, not at all. As I mentioned before, I'm an exorcist. I do not hunt demons. My main concern is for the people who are being tormented by demons and also for the souls who are trapped inside of a possessed, lifeless body. I work to relieve them of the torment; that is all."

"Wait, what do you mean by souls that are trapped?" asked Declan as widened.

"When a demon possesses someone, they will try to break them either with horrific images or physical torture. If the will of the victim is too strong for the demon to break, then eventually, they get tortured to death by the demon. The demon then has full control of the body, but the soul of the victim is stuck in the body until the demon leaves. Some demons prefer to kill their victims so that they have full control over their hosts, but it leaves them in a weakened state because they don't have full access to their powers in a lifeless body," Victor explained.

"Why don't they have full access to their powers?"

"Well, at the end of the day, they are using a body that is not theirs. It's like wearing a shirt that doesn't fit. You can't expect an Olympian to perform at their best when they are wearing ill-fitted clothing. But if they are able to break the will of their hosts, then they can just force their hosts to do their bidding while lending their abilities to the hosts," Victor further explained.

"Okay, so ... you're not a hunter. What is a hunter?" asked Declan, intrigued by the new world of supernatural entities.

"The Hunters are a group of misguided individuals who devote their lives to hunting down demons. They have learned of ways to weaken a demon, and they use these skills to hunt down someone who is possessed."

"So... why do you call the hunters misguided? It seems like they are in the same industry you are," asked Declan accusingly.

"No, they are not! Most of the demon possessed they hunt down wind up dead!" replied Victor with even more anger. "They use their limited knowledge about how to weaken the demon, the victim ends up dead, and the demon escapes! They refuse to listen when we try to explain to them why their methods only make matters worse!"

With a sudden sense of understanding, Declan said, "The victims end up dead because the hunters drown them ..."

"And sometimes they electrocute them. Yes, the running water or electricity would temporarily disable the demon, but once the body is out of the running water, the demon escapes and finds a new host. Thus, increasing the victim counts," responded Victor with even more anger in his voice.

"But wouldn't the hunters see the demons leaving the corpses and realize that their methods aren't working?" asked Declan.

"See the demon leaving?" asked Victor confused.

"Yeah, when the demon knocked me backward, I saw it come out of the Kyle, and it flew directly toward me."

Victor's eyes widened. "You saw the demon? That's impossible!"

Now it was Declan's turn to be confused. "What do you mean? You said you saw the demon push me backward."

"No, I saw you fly backward, and I had assumed that it was what had happened. In my entire career, I have never been able to physically see a demon. While in direct contact with a demon, I was given hallucinations that I had to overcome, but never directly seen them," declared Victor still sounding surprised. At first, Victor didn't believe that Declan could actually have seen the demon, but he remembered Declan raising his arms to shield himself right before he was shoved backward.

"So how do you know that the demons escaped? How do you know that it's not just hanging around right now?" asked Declan with a little bit of nervousness in his voice.

Trying to put Declan back at ease, Victor said, "Although I've never been able to see the actual demons I exorcise, I can feel it when they are around. So, don't worry. We are still safe here."

Now reassured of their safety, Declan went back into an inquisitive mood, "So ... if you guys can feel the presence of a demon, why couldn't the hunters realize that they weren't really capable of putting down the demon?"

"Declan, I really don't know why the hunters do the things they do, or what they know or do not know!"

"So why don't they just —"

"I'm sorry Declan, I know that you have a lot of questions, but I need to report back that this location has been compromised. Since you are not possessed I see no reason to keep you here. I still find your 'abilities' curious, though. How about you come back in the morning, and we can talk some more?" declared Victor, and he hurried off into the office of the house.

CHAPTER 18
-DECLAN-

Declan left the safe house with many questions on his mind. He still had a hard time believing that there were demons in the world.

Why are there demons? Where did they come from? And what do they want with us? Why would my mother know that demons must be drowned? Why could I do things that only the demon possessed could do?

Those thoughts were rampant in his mind, and he knew that if he kept thinking about it, it would drive him insane. He closed his eyes and took a deep breath.

As he walked into the streets, he realized that he knew the neighborhood. Caleb's ex-girlfriend used to attend the private school down the road, and they had carpooled together to and from school. He was on Tilden Road on the edge of Winter Garden and Windermere. He wondered if he should call his friends to come pick him up. He was, at least, four or five miles away from home. But how would he explain how he had gotten there? He didn't want to lie to his friends, so he decided that he'd just run home.

It shouldn't take me long to run five miles, anyway. I do it all the time at the gym.

Then, suddenly an idea hit him. If all those times that he was able to move at inhuman speeds were not hallucinations, then maybe he'd be able to tap into that energy again and be home in no time. Declan started to run. He ran fast, but he wouldn't have called it inhuman speed.

What am I doing wrong? How do I tap into that energy?

Declan stopped and closed his eyes. He thought about the time when he and his friends were at the club the other night and the club owner tried to prevent them from leaving. Suddenly, deep within his chest, Declan felt something thrumming, and he knew that it was the energy within. He visualized the thrumming moving from his chest down into his legs, and he started running again. This time, the street lights around him blurred into streaks of lights, and before he knew it, he stood in front of his house. He looked at his watch and only a minute had passed.

Whoa, I'm like the Flash!

Excitement exploded inside of him and his heart raced.

I wonder what else I could do.

He knew that the energy within made him faster and stronger, so he decided to test out his strength next. He walked over to his car, and he closed his eyes; visualizing the thrumming within him moving into his arms, he placed his hands underneath his car and lifted. The car practically felt weightless to him. He removed his right hand and easily kept the car lifted with just his left hand. He put his car back down and stared at his hands with amazement.

If super speed and strength are also real ...

He concentrated on his car, and within a few seconds, his car floated up into the air. He was shocked to see that it had worked. He quickly lowered his car back down to the ground.

Real! It was all real! I was never hallucinating! I was never losing it! I am not going to be like my mother!

He was so caught up in the excitement that he realized that he hadn't noticed Caleb's car parked on the side of the street. He didn't even look around to see if there was anyone who could have seen him pick up his car. He quickly looked around but didn't see anyone. He then walked toward the front door of his house and was about to insert his key when the door opened as Keira walked out.

How does she always do that? She always knows when I'm at the door.

"Deck! You're back! Oh, thank God!" exclaimed Keira as he practically jumped out of the door and embraced him.

All this time, I've been holding myself back because I was so afraid that I was losing it. But I now know the truth!

He hugged her back, fully giving into the hug as he had never done before. "Oh Keira, I have so many things ..." Declan said as Caleb interrupted him with a few coughing sounds. Declan quickly let go of Keira.

"Uh... dude, we tried calling you to check on Nelly, but you didn't answer your phone," muttered Caleb right behind Keira with a tone of mild irritation.

"Sorry, guys. I must have left my cell back at the center."

"So ... how's Nelly doing?" asked Keira finally recovering from Declan's embrace.

"Well ... uh ... when I left the hospital he was still unconscious ... Let me call Joe to find out if his condition has changed since I ... um ... left," replied Declan trying to figure out how long it had been since Victor kidnapped him from the center.

Keira and Caleb gave each other a look. "Hey Deck, are you doing okay? You look confused," asked Caleb, concerned.

"I'm fine, it's just been a really long day."

Declan was feeling guilty about having to hide the events of the exorcism today from his friends.

How can I possibly explain the situation to them? Would they even believe? I really need to figure out my story first.

"That's understandable. Is there anything we can do?" asked Keira as she warmly placed her hand onto Declan's.

"No, you guys should go home and rest up. We can go and visit Nelly together tomorrow," said Declan as he hurried his friends out.

"Deck, we're here for you. If there's anything that's bothering you, we can face it together," declared Keira as she stared sincerely into his eyes.

"Yeah, dude, you're like a brother to me. You don't have to go through anything alone. Is there anything you'd like to talk about?" asked Caleb, once again uncharacteristically serious.

"Did you guys ever find the Sullivans?" asked Declan trying to change the subject.

"We couldn't find them back in the cabin, so Caleb gave Zoe a call. She just said that something urgent came up, and she had to go back to New York really quickly. So, they called a limo to pick them up from the park. She said she'd be back in a few days," said Keira, but she realized that Declan had purposely changed the subject.

Keira gave Declan a defeated look. "Okay then, we'll see you tomorrow morning."

As Keira and Caleb started walking toward their car, Declan called out to Keira. "Keira? Can we talk privately tomorrow?"

"Um, sure Declan," replied Keira stunned. *He's never asked to speak with me alone before… and that hug just now…*

"Great!" Declan replied and walked into the house to see that his aunt and uncle were awake. "Hey, guys! What are you guys doing still up?" asked Declan as he saw the stern look on his aunt's face and realized that he was in trouble.

"Hey son, how are you doing?" asked Roy in a cautious tone as he side-glanced at Jenny. Roy and Jenny had heard about what happened earlier in the night with the ranger going insane and decided to give Declan all the support he needed. When Declan was a child, he would tell them everything that was going on, and they would help him solve his problems together. However, as he became a teenager, Declan became more reserved. He internalized his issues because he wanted to look strong to everyone, but he was too honest of a person, and his pain usually showed itself.

"I'm fine. Just about to go to bed," replied Declan trying to sound nonchalant as he quickly walked toward his room.

Jenny got up to intercept him. "How are you really doin', boy?" she asked as her eyes met his.

Oh gosh, I'm going to have to get out of this conversation! Fake a fight!

"I'm fine, why does everyone keep asking me that? As if I'm some emotionally unstable teen. I'm fine. I can cope with life. I don't need to talk about everything! Please, just leave me alone! I can deal with my own problems." Declan realized that it sounded a little more like he was throwing a tantrum than he was going for.

"Declan Peters! You watch your tone there, boy! We've been trying to reach you all night after hearing about the incident and we were worr'ed sick 'bout ya. We love you too much to deserve such treatment!" demanded Jenny glowering at Declan.

Declan, feeling guilty about hurting his aunt, walked her over to where his uncle was sitting and sat down between the two. "I'm sorry, Uncle and Auntie. I'm just really tired and frustrated by the way everyone treats me. I'm not some porcelain doll that would just break whenever life hits it."

Declan gently placed his hand on his aunt Jenny's.

"Deck, you know that we only ask if you are okay, because we care. We don't think that you are weak or unstable, we just want you to know that we love you, and we care about you," declared Roy putting his arm around him.

"I know that, Uncle. And I'm grateful for having you guys in my life. But there are just some things that I need to face myself. Can you understand that?" pleaded Declan as he moved his uncle's arm from his shoulder.

"Deck, just know that we'll always be here for ya. If you're ever facin' somethin' that is too big for ya to handle alone, we'll be here," Jenny took hold of Declan's hand.

Declan stood up and walked toward his room again, and before he exited the living room, he turned and said, "I know you guys are always going to be there for me, and I love you guys for that."

CHAPTER 19
-TRISTAN-

Tristan walked up to the front steps of his family mansion in the Hamptons. The mansion loomed over him like a mountain as he reminisced about his childhood.

I never thought about how big home was. Home ... Is this place still home if everyone you have ever cared about no longer resides here?

As he approached, the front door opened. Vin appeared in the doorway. "Welcome home young Master Tristan. I heard that the bodies have been confirmed. I am so sorry for your loss. Should I let Miss —"

"Yeah, yeah, yeah, get out of my way. I'll get them back ..." said Tristan with a tone of annoyance in his voice as he cut Vin off. Tristan quickly walked past Vin toward the basement, leaving Vin with a startled and horrified expression on his face.

Get them back? Vin shuddered. *What does he mean by that?*

The Sullivan Mansion was kept pristine by the staff. Although, the staff at the mansion was smaller than most of the staff at any other estates its size, it was the most well-kept. Apparently, fear was a good motivator.

Unlike the rest of the families in the Hamptons who constantly held parties and galleries to show off their wealth, the Sullivans seldom had visitors. Their home was easily one of the most luxurious in the Hamptons, but no one would know. The entire house was laid with marble floors with a few inlays made of precious gems. The house was filled with paintings that could rival some of the most famous paintings in the Louvre in Paris. The furniture was custom made by private designers making each piece one of a kind.

Tristan quickly moved past the foyer that was the size of a regular movie theatre. In the center of the foyer hung a huge diamond chandelier that could be sold to purchase a small nation. Through the kitchen that was equipped to cater a large wedding, Tristan strolled, turning left as he exited. Tristan got to the door of the basement and placed his hand on the hand scanner. "Print recognition confirmed. Welcome, young Master Sullivan," said a voice through the speaker on top of the hand scanner. The door opened, and he entered a dark hallway that led into a stone staircase leading down to something that looked like a cavern. As he continued down the stairway, he could hear faint echoes of running water.

When he reached the end of the staircase, there was a chasm that was fifty feet across. Tristan took a few strides, leaped across the chasm and landed on a precise narrow strip of stone that led into the holding room. This was an additional security measure that had been installed by the late Sullivan seniors in case someone was able to hack the initial hand scanner. Without the abilities like that of the Sullivan family, it would be very difficult to cross the chasm. In addition, if someone was to land in any area other than the particular narrow strip of stone, they would have fallen into the chasm as that was the only piece of solid flooring. The other strips of stone were just a holographic projection.

The last security measure that was put into place was at the door of the holding room. As Tristan approached, he felt little tingles all around him as the biometric scanner started confirming his identity. Then the door opened and said, "Welcome, young Master Tristan." As Tristan entered, the door closed behind him.

The holding room looked like a warehouse. Instead of typical shelving, there were rows and rows of running channels of water. The water flowed across rows of submerged glass jars that contained a label in front of each. Tristan walked toward the jar labeled Nergal. Eying it carefully, he pushed a button near the jar, and it rose above the surface of the water. He started a timer set for five minutes and placed his hand on the top of the jar. A transparent shape appeared in front of him like a hologram.

The shape appeared in a humanoid form, but the head looked like that of a bird. Although it had a beak, sharp razor teeth showed when the beak opened. The form had vertical slit eyes like that of a snake but glowed red. Heavy armor hung on the body that had spikes coming out as if starving to taste the blood of anyone who dared to be close enough and be impaled by them.

"Nergal, how are you enjoying your captivity?" asked Tristan snidely.

"Treacherous brat! If you've come to gloat, save it! Leave me in peace!" demanded Nergal in a shrieking raspy voice.

"No, I was merely wondering if you would like to leave," replied Tristan nonchalantly. At the sound of that, the shape's eyes glowed red.

"I'm assuming that it's an offer?" asked Nergal menacingly and drooling at the mouth.

"Yes. I will free you if you find someone for me and answer three of my questions. As chief of the demonic spies, it should be an easy task for you to locate a simple human. And you do seem to have the answers to many secrets." Tristan gave Nergal his best steely gaze.

Nergal gave a chuckle with his raspy voice, and it made Tristan's skin crawl. "So it's back to that again? What makes you think I would give you any useful information about Atlantis if I wouldn't even deal with your traitorous parents?" replied Nergal rhetorically.

"I don't care about Atlantis. That was their agenda, not mine. I swear upon my name that I will not ask you any questions regarding Atlantis. I only need you to help me find someone and answer questions regarding my family," Tristan declared staring straight into those red glowing eyes.

"Is that all you want? Oh, I bet you are just dying to find out what your treacherous parents have done. Oh, I can tell you all about their acts of treason against our king. But, I think I'll get more out of just watching you suffer in your ignorance," replied Nergal with an even louder raspy cackle than before.

"Lies! My parents have nothing to do with your king!"

The glowing red eyes of the demon widened and he sounded incredulous as he asked, "Are you really that ignorant?"

"Forget about the deal. All I'll get are lies anyway," said Tristan. He was about to remove his hand from the top of the jar when Nergal spoke, "Fine, I'll help you track down your pathetic human and answer three questions from you, but I will only give yes or no answers."

Tristan grinned. *He fell for my bluff.*

"I will need some insurance though. One, you need to swear upon your name that you will not attempt retribution against my family and me. Two, you need to swear upon your name that you will not divulge any information regarding me, my family, or this place to anyone else. And three, swear upon your name that you will answer my three questions truthfully. Do we have a deal?" asked Tristan.

"Agreed. I swear it upon my name. Now let me out of this damn jar!" demanded Nergal impatiently.

Tristan grabbed the top of the jar and lifted it out of the water, setting it down next to him on the dry ground. Now that the jar was out of the water a set of skeletal remains could be seen through its side. Tristan opened the lid and the image of Nergal disappeared as his contact with the jar ceased. Then out came a writhing shade. The image of Nergal reappeared, not as a mere transparent shape but more solid and defined.

"Now demon, answer my questions as we agreed. First question, are my parents demons?" asked Tristan.

"Yes," replied Nergal with a grin on his face.

Tristan's heart sank. Even though he had already gathered as much, it hurt him to hear it confirmed.

"Second question, were they my biological parents?" asked Tristan tensing his body as he asked, afraid of what the answer might be.

"Yes," replied Nergal with an even wider grin this time.

"Third question, what am I?" asked Tristan rashly.

"Nah uh, that's not what our agreement was. You can only ask yes or no questions," Nergal reminded him with a snicker in his voice.

"Am I also some sort of demon, then?" asked Tristan nervously.

"No," replied Nergal with his raspy voice.

Relief showed clearly on Tristan's face as his jaw unclenched. Undisturbed by the sudden change in Tristan's expression, Nergal continued, "Now, I've answered your three questions. Tell me, who do you need me to find so that we can get this over with."

Tristan took a second to answer. "I don't have his name, just an image of him in my mind."

Nergal looked at Tristan with annoyance. He reached over and placed his hand on Tristan's head for a second and said, "Got it. This will be easy. I will let you know of this man's location within an hour. After that, if we cross paths again, I will kill you."

"You swore upon your name that you will not take retribution," demanded Tristan.

With that, Nergal laughed; it sounded like metal scraping against a chalkboard. "I swore that I won't take retribution for what you've done in the past, but I am a demon after all; I don't need a reason to kill someone," replied Nergal with an even more maniacal laugh, and he disappeared.

Damn! I hate demons! If my parents are demons, but I'm not, then what the hell am I?

CHAPTER 20
-DECLAN-

"We have to get him into the lake; running water washes away his powers," shouted Tristan's voice, "If he's not fully submerged, he will escape again!"

Declan felt Tristan's hand push his head underneath the water. Out of panic, Declan breathed in the water and started to suffocate.

Declan awoke, sitting up immediately with a gasp. He realized that he was covered in sweat, and he turned to look at the clock on his nightstand. Five-thirty, he had only been asleep for an hour. Remembering the events of the previous evening made Declan's heart pound quickly and made him wonder if it had all been a dream. He went to the bathroom to wash his face and clear his mind, but the reality of Tristan's words dawned on him.

Running water washes away his powers? Declan thought in horror. *Oh, my God, I need to let Victor know.*

Without changing out of his pajamas, Declan ran out the door, got into his car, and drove to Victor's no longer "safe house."

The area that the "safe house" was located in used to be a nice area where people spent hours each week taking care of their property. In recent years, however, the market became flooded with foreclosures and short sales. Some of the surrounding houses looked like mini-jungles, and apparent property damage made the entire neighborhood look dangerous.

Declan ran up to the door. He rang the doorbell while knocking loudly at the same time. The lights inside the house lit up. Victor came to the door, apparently not having slept yet.

"Declan, I know I told you to come back in the morning, but —"

"I need you to come with me. You have another exorcism to perform," demanded Declan almost ready to grab Victor's arm and drag him out.

"What are you talking about?" asked Victor, confused by Declan's sudden urgency.

"The reason why I was at the center last night was because a friend of mine seemed to have lost his mind. He started attacking another one of my friends. The only way we were able to stop him was by holding him down in the lake." Declan explained as he gasped for air when he realized that he forgot to breathe.

"Wait a minute, Declan. Holding someone down in the water will stop anyone. What makes you say that this friend of yours was possessed?"

"He was very strong and fast. But all of that subsided once he was in the lake."

"How did you know to do that?" asked Victor, once again suspicious.

This question made Declan halt for a second, and he said, "I didn't know to do that. It was Tristan ... I think my friend might be a hunter."

Victor couldn't help but have a feeling that he was walking into a trap now that his safe house was compromised. With that, he took out the flask of holy water that was in his pocket and splashed it in Declan's face.

"Ouch! What the hell man?" screamed Declan angrily.

"I'm not falling for your tricks, demon," said Victor and took out his Taser.

"Dude! What is your deal? I thought we established that I wasn't a demon last night," demanded Declan.

"Then why did you scream in agony when I hit you with the holy water," asked Victor still holding the Taser at the ready.

"You splashed it in my eyes! Paranoid much?" yelled Declan irritably.

"Oh, that's right. I thought I had used too much salt this time in the holy water. Sorry, I just had to make sure." Victor reached one hand out to help Declan up.

"Can you please put away the Taser?"

Victor realized that he still had the Taser in his other hand pointed at Declan and quickly put it away.

"Do you believe me now? Will you help my friend?" pleaded Declan.

Victor looked at his watch and said, "Fine, I'll examine your friend. If he's truly possessed, then I'll perform the exorcism."

"You can just do it there? Why did you kidnap Kyle and I last night?"

"There's a lot of work that goes into securing the location so that when the demon is exorcised it doesn't escape. That's why we set up safe houses; they already have all the preparations that make it safe to perform the exorcism. However, it is now the morning. It is much more difficult to kidnap a patient during the daytime," said Victor with a hint of annoyance.

"Fine, let's get going then with the examination," Declan demanded and signaled toward his car.

"If you want me to do this, you're going to have to help. Like I said, it's a lot of work getting a location secured. And also, you're going to have to keep a lookout in case someone passes by," warned Victor.

Victor walked out of the house, turned around and locked the door. "Is Kyle going to be safe in the house all alone, since it's been 'compromised'?" asked Declan as he opened the car door to the driver's seat.

"I've been blessing all the walls and entrances of the house since you left. It's safe from any demons for now."

ॐ☯ॐ

"Since we've got some time before we arrive at the center, I have a few more questions," said Declan grinning sheepishly.

Victor rolled his eyes and said with annoyance in his voice, "I haven't slept yet. I was hoping to get some shut-eye in the car ... but fine, ask away."

"Great! Okay, so ... why do demons possess people?" asked Declan excitedly.

"I thought that I had already talked about this before." Victor with growing annoyance, begrudgingly continued to explain, "Demons are spirits. Without a physical body, they cannot interact with the physical world. Therefore, they possess humans to once again experience life."

Declan looked pensively for a moment and asked, "I'm confused, you say that they are spirits, so ... you mean they're ghosts?"

Declan's question made Victor frown. "It's a long story. Are you familiar with the Bible?"

"I guess ... I don't really believe in it, though. I did grow up going to Sunday school because my aunt and uncle made me," replied Declan with resentment in his voice.

"What can you tell me about the flood in Genesis?" asked Victor sounding like a schoolteacher.

"Like, 'The Flood'? Like, the flood and Noah's Ark?" asked Declan. Victor nodded. Declan continued, "Well ... people on the earth became so wicked, God decided to wipe out mankind with the exception of Noah because he was blameless."

Victor's eyebrow rose, "Hmm ... blameless ... from the context of the rest of the Bible. Has there been anyone else, other than the Lord

Jesus Christ, who has been blameless? And Noah wasn't the only one who was saved, right? Noah's entire family was saved."

Declan had to think about that for a minute. "No, I guess not. We were taught that all have sinned and fallen short of the glory of God. But then didn't the Bible just contradict itself?" asked Declan smugly. He'd been waiting to find a contradiction in the Bible since he was a teenager.

"No, there is no contradiction there. The problem is translation and interpretation. The Hebrew word translated to blameless in the Bible version you learned from is *tamiym*, which is closer to 'without blemish.' So when the Bible said that Noah was blameless among his generation, another way to translate that is that he was without blemish in his gene pool," replied Victor.

"What?! That is such a stretch! I've never heard anyone translate it that way before. I thought it was wrong to bend the words of scripture," said Declan cynically with a grin toward Victor.

"You have to read your Bible in context. You paraphrased Genesis 6:9. Did you even pay attention to what was going on in verses 1-8?" asked Victor prodding on.

Declan scratched his head, "I don't know, I've only heard the story being told, I've never really read it myself."

Victor pulled out a NIV Bible from his pocket and read aloud to Declan, "Genesis six, verse four, 'The Nephilim were on the earth in those days-and also afterward-when the sons of God went to the daughter of humans and had children by them. They were the heroes of old, men of renown.' Do you understand what was going on? Do you know who the sons of God were?"

"Aren't we all considered children of God?" asked Declan confused.

"Yes, but the term used in Genesis here is specifically a term used for angels," replied Victor with a bit of excitement in his voice.

"Wait, are you telling me that angels were having babies with people? That's really strange. I thought that Jesus said that angels didn't get married when he was asked about who'd be married to whom in heaven in the example of the girl with multiple husbands?" asked Declan smugly.

"So you do know your Bible stories pretty well. Yes, the Lord did say that they didn't marry, but said nothing about them not being able to have children. I'm sure you've watched Jerry Springer before right? You don't have to be married to be someone's baby daddy." Victor smirked.

"You did not just say 'baby daddy?' Wow ..." Declan rolled his eyes.

Ignoring Declan's comment, Victor continued. "So eventually, the human bloodline got mixed with angels and, well, people tend to abuse powers. So as you said, things got so bad, the Lord decided to wipeout mankind, but he found Noah to be without blemish in his gene pool. Therefore, Noah and his bloodline were preserved. You see, no contradiction."

"Okay, even if I buy into your crazy interpretation of the story of Noah's Ark, it still doesn't explain anything about demons," stated Declan defiantly.

"Well, you need to then look at the *Book of Enoch*, chapter fifteen," answered Victor once again with a smirk on his face.

"There is no *Book of Enoch* in the Bible. I'm sure of that," declared Declan smugly.

"No, the *Book of Enoch* was not part of the canon, but just because it wasn't considered inspired doesn't mean that it couldn't contain some level of truth to it."

"Wait one second, I thought 'you people' don't believe in anything that's not written in the Bible," said Declan in a mocking tone.

"No, we just believe everything in the Bible to be true, but that doesn't exclude truth from anything outside of the Bible. And what do you mean by you people?" asked Victor sounding offended.

"You know, Christians!" exclaimed Declan.

"Oh, and we're considered the intolerant ones. You just stereotyped millions of people. But anyway, let me go back to my explanation. According to chapter fifteen of the *Book of Enoch*, after the flood wiped out all the Nephilim, they became the evil spirits of the earth, demons. So in a sense, yes, they are the ghosts of the Nephilim."

Declan's jaw dropped open. "So ... what you are telling me is that there were human and angel hybrids? When they died and became ghosts, they became demons?" Declan asked, eyes widening.

Victor grinned. "In my opinion, they probably came back as demons even before the flood. There has always been a decree to eliminate the Nephilim. They were abominations, being human-angel hybrids. But they kept coming back as demons and possessing people. We might seem to be the dominant species, but in reality, we die pretty easily. There were many ways the Lord could have wiped out the tainted human race. I don't think that it was just a coincidence that the Lord chose drowning," said Victor.

CHAPTER 21
-DECLAN-

Declan pulled the car into the employee parking lot of his work place. He stayed quiet as they went into the center and into the locker room to change into their UAP uniforms. He was thinking about the conversation they'd been having in the car.

Why do I have access to abilities that demons have? But I'm not demon possessed. Does that mean that I'm a Nephilim? Maybe I was somehow switched at birth at the hospital, and one of my parents was actually an angel. That's not possible since my aunt constantly tells me how much I look like my dad. And since my aunt is ... definitely not an angel, my dad can't possibly be an angel. That leaves my mom ...

He couldn't help but laugh to himself when he thought that his crazy mother could possibly have been an angel.

They changed into their white uniforms and headed toward the fifth floor where Nelly was most likely sent. They used the floor computer to figure out which room Nelly was in and off they went trying not to look too suspicious. When they reached the room, Nelly hadn't regained consciousness.

"So ... how are you going to determine if he's possessed or not, just pour holy water on him?" asked Declan.

"Nope. He's unconscious. Can't do anything unless he's conscious." Victor looked at Declan, expecting the flood of questions.

"What? Why?" asked Declan looking confused.

"It's hard to explain. You would think that a person was most vulnerable when they are asleep. Yes, that might be true in the physical sense; but in the spiritual sense, that is the opposite. A person's spirit is strongest when they are unconscious. As a matter of fact, a person's spirit completely suppresses a demon when he or she is unconscious. That's why when I took Kyle back to the safe house the demon couldn't escape; it was basically powerless while Kyle was unconscious. So at the same time, things that would normally harm it also have no effect," explained Victor.

"So… what do we do? Wait for him to wake up?" asked Declan impatiently.

Victor reached into his pocket and took out his bottle of holy water. "It doesn't hurt to be prepared," said Victor as he started praying, "Heavenly Father, please lend us your strength today as we gather in this room to exorcise the unclean spirit from Your child. Surround the walls of this room with Your power so that there will be no escape for what is evil. Protect us whilst we are in this room and protect that which has been afflicted with the unclean spirit so that no further harm may come of him. We pray these things in the name of Your Son, Jesus Christ. Amen."

As Victor completed his prayer, Declan felt a strange sensation cover him like a warm blanket. A sense of peace overwhelmed him, and he felt at ease. Victor directed Declan to splash the four walls of the room with holy water. He continued to do the same with the ceiling and the floor. Then he walked over to Nelly and overlaid the arm and leg restraints with rosaries.

"You just keep all that stuff on you all the time?" asked Declan mockingly. He continued, "What else do you have in those pockets?"

Victor smiled and said, "Once again, it doesn't hurt to be prepared."

Just then, Nelly started to stir. Declan's eyes quickly darted in Nelly's direction.

Remaining perfectly still, Nelly asked, "Declan? What's going on? Why am I tied up?"

Declan had expected violent screams and struggles from Nelly as he awoke, but he was taken aback by how lucid he was. He felt relieved by Nelly's reaction. Although the whole idea of the exorcism was intriguing to Declan, he also had some fears about participating. Declan quickly walked over to Nelly's side and asked, "You don't remember what happened last night?"

"Last night?" asked Nelly sounding confused. He continued, "No, I worked during the day and went to bed as I normally do. Where is this place? Why am I tied up?"

"Oh Nelly, I don't know how to tell you this, but you attacked a friend of mine last night. I think the stress might have gotten to you, and something snapped. We had to hospitalize you; it was for your own safety," explained Declan finding it hard to tell Nelly about his circumstances.

Nelly looked upset about the whole situation. Then he looked down at his wrists. "Hey, Declan. I can see that you had to restrain me, but what's the deal with the rosaries? You know that I'm not religious. Do these belong to that silly girlfriend of yours?"

Declan's face started to flush red. "Keira's not my girlfriend ...," He started to take the rosaries off the restraints when Victor stopped him by placing a hand on his. Declan looked up at Victor confused. "I think he's alright now. I mean ... he seems like himself again."

"Yes, I feel fine now. Get those rosaries off me. You know how I hate it when Keira pushes her religion on me," said Nelly hastily with a bit of snarl in his voice.

Declan could relate. Keira was always preaching to him about Jesus, and it had also irritated him. He went back to untangling the rosary, but Victor pushed him back. Victor took the crucifix end of the rosary and pressed it into Nelly's arm. Nelly screamed immediately with a roar that didn't sound like his voice. He started pulling on the restraints on his wrists so hard that he started to bleed.

"I will kill you, old man!" screamed Nelly, and the rage in his eyes was menacing.

Declan jumped back in shock at what he just saw. That roar that came out of Nelly was so horrific that Declan was almost paralyzed with fear.

Victor splashed some holy water on Nelly, and Nelly screamed again. "Silence you vile creature," demanded Victor, and started praying again.

"Our Father who art in heaven, hallowed be Thy name. Thy kingdom come; Thy will be done here on earth as it is in heaven. Give us this day our daily bread and forgive us our trespasses as we forgive those who trespass against us. And lead us not into temptation, but deliver us from evil."

"Deliver us from evil," mocked Nelly, "What's evil is in the hearts of man. You need deliverance from yourselves."

Victor ignored Nelly, splashing more holy water on him, making Nelly writhe in agony.

Victor continued, "The Lord is my shepherd; I shall not want. He maketh me to lie down in green pastures: He leadeth me beside the still waters. He restoreth my soul: He leadeth me in the paths of righteousness for His name's sake. Yea, though I walk through the valley of the shadow of death..."

"Death is all you will ever find when I get out of here. I will hunt you down like sheep you son of a bi—" Nelly screamed, but another splash of holy water shut him up.

Again Victor continued, "I will fear no evil: for Thou art with me; Thy rod and Thy staff they comfort me. Thou prepares a table before me in the presence of mine enemies: Thou anoints my head with oil; my cup runneth over. Surely goodness and mercy shall follow me all the days of my life: and I will dwell in the house of the Lord forever."

In an attempt to disrupt Victor again, Nelly bit his own tongue and spat blood all over Victor. Declan's eyes widened as he saw all the blood that was trickling down Nelly's wrists from the struggles with the restraints, and the blood that was now covering Victor. Victor, however, wasn't fazed. He continued on, "I command you, unclean spirit, whoever you are, along with all your minions now attacking this servant of God, by the mysteries of the incarnation, passion, resurrection, and ascension of our Lord Jesus Christ, by the descent of the Holy Spirit, by the coming of our Lord for judgment, that you tell me your name."

Again to disrupt Victor's flow, Nelly made more obscene comments and this time started to arch his back so much that it looked as if Nelly's back was broken. Victor splashed more holy water on Nelly and this time placed a crucifix on top of his midsection forcing him back down.

Victor yelled now with anger in his voice, "Declan come help me hold him down."

Declan snapped out of his shock. He quickly ran over and did as he was told. As soon as he made contact with Nelly, coldness spread up from his hands and to the rest of his body. The feeling of overwhelming gloom consumed him.

This is hopeless. I've lost my mind, and I'm going to end up murdering my friends and family. My mother should have killed me when she had the chance. All I'll ever do is cause sorrow.

Victor splashed Declan's face with holy water, pulling Declan out of his gloom. "Snap out of it. The demon is manipulating your thoughts! Resist him!" Victor yelled into Declan's ear.

Victor continued with even more anger in his voice, "I command you to obey me to the letter. I am a minister of God despite my unworthiness. You shall not be emboldened to harm in any way this creature of God, or the bystanders, or any of their possessions. By the name of the Lord Jesus Christ heed my commands!"

Victor made the sign of the cross on Nelly's forehead and Nelly writhed even more while Victor prayed, "God and Father of our Lord Jesus Christ, I appeal to your holy name, humbly begging your kindness, that you graciously grant me help against this and every unclean spirit now tormenting this creature of Yours; through Christ our Lord."

Nelly was now resisting so much that Declan had to put his full strength into holding him down. Once again, Declan felt ice against his hand threatening to spread up his body. He quickly reached deep inside for the thrumming he felt and pushed the thrumming against the coldness. He saw his arms glow red, and the ice that he felt against his hands faded. Nelly continued to spit blood all over the place, and soon Declan was also drenched in Nelly's blood.

"Vile spirit, in the name of Christ Jesus, reveal your name," demanded Victor.

Nelly pulled his lips together to force his mouth shut, glaring at Victor with mad fury.

Victor repeated his previous demand, and Nelly had to bite down on his lips to keep them sealed. Blood trickled from his lips as Nelly bit through his lips in an effort to keep his mouth from opening, but he couldn't help himself and yelled, "Vetis!"

Victor then commanded, "Vetis, I command you in the name of Jesus Christ, the Lord of lords and King of kings, to keep silent and allow me to speak to your host.

All of a sudden, the expression of anger disappeared from Nelly's face, instead, an expression of fear appeared. Tears started to roll out of Nelly's eyes, and he was hyperventilating.

"D ... D ... Declan? Is that you? Please help me! Please!" cried Nelly.

"Listen to me, Nelly, you have been under demonic attack," explained Victor.

"I know," cried Nelly with more tears rolling out of his eyes.

"I am currently performing an exorcism to rid you of this demonic presence, but from this point forward I will need your help. I cannot remove this demon from your body for you; you have to want it yourself. Cry out to the Lord Jesus Christ for help, and it shall be given to you. Do you understand?" asked Victor.

"Y ... Yes. Please help me Jesus," Nelly cried with blood still coming out of his mouth and wrists.

In a commanding voice, Victor said, "I cast you out, Vetis, in the name of our Lord Jesus Christ, who lives and reigns with the Father and the Holy Spirit, God, forever and ever. Be gone and stay far from this creature of God."

Nelly screamed out again with the most agonizing pain as his voice changed back and forth between his own and a deafening growl. Once again, Declan saw a shade crawl out, he became so terrified that he flinched from it as it was expelled from Nelly's body. The shade started zooming all across the room but recoiled after hitting one of the walls.

Victor held up a small metallic test tube looking vial and declared, "Vetis, in the name of the Most High God, in the form of His one and only Begotten Son, Jesus Christ, I bind you to this vial. May you be bound to this vial until the day you are cast into the eternal lake of fire, so that you may no longer do harm to God's children."

And with that, it looked as if there was a vortex that formed from within the vial and drew the shade into it. Victor put a twist cap on the vial and wrapped it with a cloth with a crucifix on it. Declan stared wide-eyed at Victor and the vial. Sobs coming from Nelly broke Declan's stare, and he ran over to him.

"Hey there ... welcome back. It's all over now," said Declan trying to soothe him.

Victor left the room after removing all his exorcism equipment and came back with the regular UAPs on the floor. He had told them that he and Declan were on their way to visit Declan's mother. When they passed by the patient's room, they had found the patient struggling so much against the restraints that he started bleeding. When the UAPs came in, they gave Nelly a shot of sedative while the nurses worked on bandaging his wrists and putting a mouth guard into his mouth.

Victor walked out of the room and went back to the locker room to change out of the bloody clothes. Declan followed.

"So ... what are we going to do with Nelly now?" asked Declan.

"Nothing, he's already in the best place for his care," responded Victor sadly.

"What? Why? Why couldn't he go to the rehab location where Kyle's going?" asked Declan confused.

"It's too late for him," said Victor still in his sad tone.

Getting angry at the comment, Declan asked, "What do you mean 'it's too late for him?' Why can't we help him?"

"From the looks of it, the demon had full control over Nelly. You can tell by the way he tried to get you to remove the rosaries. For a demon to exert that much control, the demon had to have already mentally broken him. I don't think he will ever be normal again," said Victor sadly without looking at Declan, but Declan saw the tears building in Victor's eyes.

CHAPTER 22
-ZOE AND TRISTAN-

"**M**ah ... mah ... Miss Zoe! Please don't go! Young Master Tristan would be most upset if you left. He's already lost your parents this week. He cannot lose you, too," pleaded Vin as Zoe stuffed her clothes into a suitcase.

"Vin, get out of my way! I can't be here anymore ... around all of this! That's not who I want to be! I want a normal life!" Zoe exclaimed as she dragged her suitcase out of her bedroom.

"You don't understand, Miss Zoe, if Master Tristan finds your room empty, he'll take it out on me!" Vin pleaded again.

"Trist is back?" asked Zoe surprised.

"Yes, but he went down into the ... basement," responded Vin with a little bit of hesitation. The basement had always scared him even though he had never gone down there. Every time the Sullivans returned from a trip, they would carry large containers down into the basement, and those containers would never be seen again. It was always done so quickly that none of the staff at the mansion had ever seen what was taken down there. No one, that is, except for Vin.

David and Lydia Sullivan had always done an excellent job at hiding their secrets from the staff. With the exception of their inhuman strength that was difficult to hide, their terrible temper and bad gas passing habits, the staff didn't know much else about David and Lydia.

However, as Tristan and Zoe became teenagers, the staff started seeing more and more strange things that the Sullivans were capable of. For example, within the past couple of years, almost all of them had seen either Tristan or Zoe move at inhuman speeds. They had also seen the teenagers having broken limbs one day and moving with perfect agility the next. There were rumors going around the staff that the Sullivans were aliens that had infiltrated their world; however, no one really believed those rumors as most of the staff had watched the teenagers grow up from infants. The staff figured that the Sullivans might not be aliens, but they were definitely not an ordinary family.

Vin would have assumed that the Sullivans were simply bad tempered people who were ridiculously strong if it weren't for the two teenagers. After the first trip that the Sullivans took their children on, they came back with two big containers. David and Lydia wanted to teach Tristan and Zoe what went on in the basement and requested the two teens to take the containers there. Competitive as the two teens always were, they had decided to race each other to the basement. Since both of them were equally fast and careless, they got to the door at the same time and bumped into each other, causing both their containers to tip over and the cover of the containers slipped off. Vin was in the hallway at the time and took a quick glimpse into the contents of one of the containers. The contents frightened him so much that he had quickly hidden behind one of the giant vases in the hall. Inside each container were two aquarium-like glass jars, one with a set of human remains and the other appeared to only have water. There were tubes that ran from one to the next that looked like they were used for circulating the water between the two jars.

"Be careful, you two! You could have released the two demons, and we'll have a real problem on our hands!" yelled David angrily.

"David, it's fine. Nothing happened. They're just kids ..." said Lydia as she grabbed hold of David's hand.

"Hello! Vin! I just asked you a question! How long has he been down there? Why didn't you tell me that Tristan came home?" demanded

Zoe jolting Vin from his memory of the basement incident. Seeing how demanding Zoe was, Vin had automatically flinched away and covered his face.

Vin's reaction shocked Zoe and her demeanor dropped. *Oh my gosh! He's afraid of me! They've always been afraid of me. I criticized Tristan for acting like a demon, but I've been the same way.*

"Vin, I just want to tell you that ... I'm sorry if I have been short with you in the past. I should have never taken my anger out on you. Now please, I don't want you to fear me. Tell me, how long has my brother been down there?" asked Zoe with the most sincere look she could muster.

Vin looked surprised, as the Sullivans had never apologized to him before. He lowered his hands from his face. "Master Tristan has been in the basement for about an hour now. He mentioned something about bringing them back ..."

Zoe, not knowing what her brother could be up to, raced down the stairs toward the basement. As she approached the door with the hand scanner, it opened, and Tristan came out.

"Zoe? I didn't know that you had come back—"

"What were you doing down there?" asked Zoe coldly as she glared at Tristan.

"I can see that you're still mad at me. I'm sorry Zoe. I never meant to hit you. I don't know what got into me. I promise that I will never do that again. Can you please forgive me?" asked Tristan sincerely.

Zoe's glare faded a second, but it regained its fervor as she said, "I don't care about that right now. What were you doing down there?"

"I have a lead on who could have done this to our parents. I needed some help ... in finding this person. Who knows, maybe we can get them back!" replied Tristan with excitement in his voice.

"You're making deals with demons?" asked Zoe with disgust in her voice.

"Don't worry, I made him swear upon his name. He's bound to the task, and he cannot retaliate," replied Tristan trying to ease Zoe's concern or what he thought was a concern.

"Tristan, you know what happens to those that make deals with demons. Demons lie!" demanded Zoe.

"I don't care, Zoe. If we can get them back, don't you think it's worth the risk? At least, we can get some answers," replied Tristan in a desperate tone that Zoe had never heard in her brother's voice before.

"Tristan, I want them back as much as you do, but this ... I don't want any part of, and I don't want this for you either," Zoe said with tears rolling out of her eyes as she hugged Tristan.

The moment was ruined as maniacal laughter came from the corner of the hall. "How sweet! Little sissy doesn't want big brother to play with the nasty demon," the raspy voice mocked.

Tristan instinctively moved between his sister and the demon and said, "Well, have you completed your task? Where is he?"

"Oh yes, I sure did. And I found out so much more, but you didn't tell me that the person you were looking for was an exorcist. For a task so dangerous, I'm going to need something a little more," said Nergal. He broke into another laugh.

"That was not our deal. You swore upon your own name. Are you backing out?" asked Tristan confidently.

"Demon, go use your tricks on someone else. We will not fall for them," said Zoe as she moved from behind Tristan to stand beside him.

"I only promised that I'd help you find him and that I would return in an hour, but I never promised when I'd reveal to you what I've found out," replied Nergal as a cackling screeching laughter came out of him.

"Damn it!" Tristan cursed, "What do you want?"

"Tristan, no!" cried Zoe as she placed a hand on his shoulder.

Nergal swarmed up to Tristan and writhed until its shadow-like body wrapped around Tristan. "Little lost boy, you've only skimmed the surface of your abilities. I can show you so much more. Have you ever channeled the powers of a demon? I can give you access to powers beyond your imagination. I can show you how to utilize your powers to your full potential. All you need to do is invite me in," Nergal whispered into Tristan's ear.

"Get away from my brother!" yelled Zoe as she grabbed hold of the transparent entity. Zoe's hands started to glow red, and it spread over her entire body.

"Zoe! No!" yelled Tristan as he grabbed hold of the demon. Tristan's hands also started to glow red, and the glow also spread over his entire body.

"Tristan, I won't let this demon swindle you into letting it use you. Let go! There's no point in both of us wasting our life force on it," pleaded Zoe as she kicked Tristan away from herself and the demon. "Powerless," Zoe said forcing her will into her words, "Come in!"

Nergal screamed as it was drawn into Zoe's body. As the demon entered Zoe, the red glow spread across her entire body.

"Be careful what you ask for, demon! You wanted a body to reside in, and now you have one. I hope you enjoy your confinement," said Zoe as she dropped down to her knees with a look of agony.

"Zoe! What have you done? Don't waste your life force on a low life demon," pleaded Tristan as he rushed over to Zoe to hold her.

"No, Tristan, not for the demon, but for you. I figured it out when we fought the demon at the club. Our auras are impenetrable to the demons. Using my powers, I can make it so that the demon cannot exert its powers on me while inside of me, while my aura keeps it from escaping," explained Zoe, her voice getting weaker.

"It's killing you! Just let it go!" Tristan continued to plead.

"If I die, my aura will continue to hold the demon. It will be confined to my body forever. I don't want you making deals with demons. Please don't do anything so foolish again," said Zoe as her voice started to sound weak and the red glow around her started to fade.

"No! I can't be locked up again! Let me out! I'll tell you what you need!" screamed Nergal.

CHAPTER 23
-DECLAN-

Declan was driving Victor back to the "safe house," looking dazed. He was still trying to work off the shock of the events of the past day. He had never seen that much blood in his life. It was a good thing he had an extra uniform in his locker. Seeing such horrors would have kept anyone dazed for a couple of days, but being a person with an inquisitive mind, Declan couldn't pass up the opportunity to ask Victor more questions.

"So … what's the deal with the little test tubes?" asked Declan, breaking the silence.

"That mind of yours never stops does it?" asked Victor looking extremely tired.

"It's just all so strange to me, but yet I feel very connected to all of this," said Declan pensively.

Victor sighed and answered, "The vials are what we use to trap the demons. The demon is now bound to this vial. Even if the cap is removed and the vial is cut in half, the demon is still bound to this vial. As long as this vial remains a vial, that demon isn't going anywhere."

"As long as it remains a vial? What do you mean by that?" asked Declan in a confused tone.

Victor sighed again, apparently annoyed with the constant questions. "Declan, you have to understand that words have power.

Because the words I had used commanded the demon to be bound to the vial, it is only bound as long as it is a vial. If the vial was melted down it would no longer be a vial, and the binding will no longer hold. That is why our vials are now made out of tungsten because it has a high melting point."

Declan thought for a minute, and Victor started to close his eyes because he thought Declan was finally done, but Declan asked again, "So, if the vial has to be melted down in order for the demon to be released, why do you even cap the vial? And why do you handle it with so much care as if you were afraid of breaking it?"

Victor squeezed his eyes tight as if he was pushing down his anger. "I can tell that you really aren't going to give me any time to sleep, are you? Fine! But, you are buying me coffee!"

Declan drove through a Dunkin Donuts drive-thru and bought two coffees and a dozen doughnuts. Victor took a big whiff of his hazelnut coffee and took a big bite from his jelly doughnut. "That's more like it. That's how you should treat your elders."

"Until this morning, you were just my kidnapper," replied Declan with a smirk.

"You didn't call me that when you asked for my help." Victor crossed his arms and glared at Declan..

"Alright, alright, I'm sorry. Can you please tell me about the capping and careful wrapping of the vials?" asked Declan raising one hand up in surrender as his other hand remained on the steering wheel.

Victor muffled with a mouthful of doughnut in response. "Because the demon is confined to the vial, it can still influence anyone that the vial comes into contact with. The vial is capped to indicate that there is a demon bound in it, and it also restricts physical contact to the interior surface of the vial. Also, we never directly touch the vials so we use a cloth that will serve as a barrier between our hand and them."

"What do you mean by influence?" asked Declan.

"Remember what happened when you tried to hold Nelly down earlier? Through contact with the vial, the demon can communicate with you and make you see anything it wishes. Where do you think the legends of genies of the lamps come from? The holder of the object that a demon is bound to is given hallucinations that wishes have been granted to them. Then the demon convinces the holder to destroy the object to set them free," Victor answered as he took a sip of his coffee and gave a sound of ecstasy.

"Aladdin was duped by a demon?" asked Declan incredulously.

"Yes he was, and later possessed by the same demon, becoming a very frightening ruler of the area he lived in," replied Victor sounding tired.

"Okay … note to self, never pick up random objects. And if a voice comes from it, ditch it and run." Declan looked nervously at Victor's pocket where the vial with the bound demon resided. "So … what do you do with the vials? They seem kind of … dangerous …"

"It's safer for you not to know this part. I don't even know the exact locations. All I know is that there are multiple locations where these vials are safely locked up. They are constantly being moved around so that they are never in one location for too long. It's for our protection that we don't know because the demons are constantly after them. If you know, you can become a target. And trust me, the demons are masters of torture, physically, mentally, and emotionally. Some of us have been forced to watch as each of our loved ones were tortured and killed in front of our eyes," explained Victor as redness and tears crept into his eyes.

ಬಂಡ

The rest of the ride back to the "safe house" was quiet, and Victor was finally able to get some sleep. When they arrived, there was a car parked in front of the house and someone was standing on the front porch. Victor quickly rushed out of the car to the man on the front porch while Declan stayed inside.

The stranger on the front porch looked to be in his early thirties, dressed in a fitted suit. He had short blonde hair, almost as if cut in a G.I. style. Despite his professional looking attire, his body language showed that he was rather relaxed and not uptight.

The two men gave each other a friendly embrace and Victor said, "Thank you for coming so quickly, Brother. Let's go inside and talk." Victor turned and waved goodbye to Declan and walked into the house.

⁝⁞⁜

Declan realized how tired he was as he drove home. He had only gotten an hour of sleep. He parked his car in front of his house, and as he got to his door, two men dressed in suits got out of a car across the street. "Declan Peters?"

Declan turned around to see who called. "Yes, can I help you?"

One of the men showed a badge to Declan. "This is Agent Warren and I'm Agent Peterson; we're from the FBI. We have a few questions to ask you."

Startled by the sudden appearance of the two agents, Declan was barely able to utter, "Um … uh … sure … would you like to come inside?"

"No, we only have a few quick questions," replied Agent Peterson impatiently.

Agent Warren took a photograph out of his pocket and handed it to Declan. "Do you know the whereabouts of the man in the photo that you were talking to?"

Declan looked at the picture of him talking to Victor in the elevator when they met.

"I … uh … have no idea where he would be. I only met him the other day. He is a new employee at the behavioral center I work at," Declan stammered as he tried to suppress his anxiety.

"We've checked. There is no record of his employment at the center," replied Agent Peterson.

A few seconds passed and Declan thought about what he would say, but Agent Warren broke the silence, "You don't seem surprised."

"Well ... I ... I" Declan responded nervously.

Agent Warren grabbed Declan by the collar and pushed him up against the front door. "What are you hiding, kid?"

Just then, Declan's front door opened and Jenny walked out. "Oh Declan have ya forgotten ya keys again?" She stopped as she noticed the two agents and demanded, "Get your filthy hands off of him! Who are ya? What do ya want from him?"

"Ma'am, we're from the FBI. We were just asking Declan some questions," replied Agent Peterson as Agent Warren released Declan.

"Oh yeah, what about?" asked Jenny in a momma bear tone as she walked out of the doorway and put herself between Declan and the agents.

Agent Warren ignored Jenny. "Kid, if you know something, you better tell us. Otherwise, we can charge you with obstruction of justice."

"I don't appreciate bein' ignored. And that there better have not been a threat," replied Jenny staring Agent Peterson right in the eyes.

"Ma'am, please excuse my colleague, but we only have a few questions we'd like to ask Declan privately," said Agent Peterson, but he was interrupted by Jenny.

"No, ya ain't," replied Jenny in the coldest tone Declan have ever heard his aunt use while she continued to stare Agent Peterson down.

"Ma'am, this has nothing to do with you —" Agent Warren started to say.

"Declan, go inside! And until you boys learn some manners, don't expect me to allow him to answer any of your questions," replied Jenny as she started walking inside the house.

Agent Warren put his foot between the door and doorframe as Jenny was closing it. "Ma'am, you can't stop us from questioning him!"

Jenny opened the door again and stood firm in the doorway staring into Agent Warren's eyes, "Do I look like an ignorant old woman? I know my Miranda Rights. Ya might think that you can use your scare tactics to make the boy believe that he has to answer your questions, but don't think that it'll work on me. Now get off mah property!"

Agent Peterson, trying to play good cop, pulled Agent Warren back. "We apologize ma'am. Nobody is being placed under arrest so there's no need to mention Miranda Rights. Please accept our apologies, but we believe that Declan might have some information that can lead us to a serial killer."

The steel in Jenny's eyes softened for a second but was restored as she said, "Since no one is bein' placed under arrest, then we here are even less obligated to answer any of your questions. Besides, I'm sure that Declan has nothin' to do with some serial killer. You boys are barkin' up the wrong tree."

"Ma'am we have pictures of Declan speaking with the suspect." Agent Peterson produced the photo to Jenny.

The maternal instincts to protect Declan overwhelmed Jenny again. "So what are ya tryin' to accuse mah boy of? So what? He was talkin' to a co-worker. That don't mean that he knows anythin'. And if I see ya harassin' mah boy, who is a minor, by the way, I'll file an official complaint. Now are ya gonna get off mah front porch or am I gonna have to remove ya?"

"If we find out that he's hiding something, ma'am, we will charge both of you for obstruction," threatened Agent Peterson as Agent Warren continued to pull him away.

Jenny gave Agent Warren the coldest stare, and said as she shut the door, "He doesn't know anything!"

Jenny walked into her living room and called out to Declan, "Declan Peters, ya get yo butt out here right fast! What kind of trouble have ya gotten yourself into?"

But there was no response. Declan had already snuck out through the backdoor.

CHAPTER 24
-DECLAN-

Declan ran toward the exorcist's safe house using one of the back streets so that he didn't run into the two agents. He knew that he needed to alert Victor about the FBI as soon as possible.

If only I could use my super speed, but I can't do that in broad daylight.

"Hey Deck!" Caleb yelled from the rolled-down window of his car as he drove up to Declan.

"Caleb? What are you doing here?"

"You said we were going to visit Nelly together at the hospital … where were you running to?" asked Caleb as the passenger seat window rolled down.

Keira stuck her head out of the window. "Get in Deck!"

Declan opened the car door and sat down in the back. "I was uh … running to your house so that we could meet up and go to the hospital together."

"Do you have to work today? Why are you in your work uniform?" asked Keira as she noticed what Declan was wearing.

"Uh … yeah, I figured that I'd pull a few extra hours for some holiday money," Declan replied quickly. "Hey, can we make a quick stop at my co-worker's house before we go to the hospital?"

"Sure… dude. I don't buy your whole holiday money story. You look like hell. You're just dressed in your work uniform so people won't think you're a patient there!" Caleb beamed as he showed a large grin at Declan through the rearview mirror.

"Ha-ha, you're so funny. Just drive! Go down Daniels Road and make a right on Tilden," replied Declan as he gave Caleb the stink eye.

"So … have you heard anything about Nelly yet?" asked Keira genuinely concerned.

"I … um … heard he had another meltdown this morning when he woke. It was messy … uh … that's why I came running toward your house," replied Declan guilty about lying to his friends, but at the same time, impressed by his ability to piece all that together.

"Poor guy … I spoke with him yesterday morning when we were renting the canoes. He had just gotten some cancerous skin removed, and he was still very shaken up about it. I wonder if it had anything to do with his meltdown," said Keira to herself, but she realized she had spoken aloud.

"What are we going to your co-worker's place for anyway?" asked Caleb as he made the turn at Tilden Rd.

"Oh, I just need to get something from him for work. I told you, I have to work today," replied Declan getting tired of making up lies.

"Why didn't you drive then? How are you getting home after work?" asked Caleb with some suspicion in his voice.

"I … was planning … to find a ride with one of my co-workers," he replied, starting to sweat.

"Oh, don't be ridiculous Deck. We'll come pick you up. We can just grab dinner together afterward," replied Keira as she waved off the notion.

"We will? You assume that I have nothing better to do on a Friday night than to hang out with my little baby sister? You never know, maybe I have a hot date or something," replied Caleb indignantly.

"Well, do you?" challenged Keira.

"Caleb, the house on the right is the one. Can you just pull over? I won't be long." Declan darted out of the car before Caleb and Keira could say another word.

⊱⊰

Declan rang the doorbell and banged on the door several times before Victor opened it. "Declan, what on earth are you doing back here again? Please, I don't have time for your silly questions right now. I've got to get everything packed up for the move."

"Wait, you have to listen to me," pleaded Declan, when he was interrupted by a voice inside the house.

"Is this the kid you were talking about earlier?" he asked as he poked his head into the light that was let in through the doorway.

"Oh, alright, come on in. Declan, meet Collin and Collin meet Declan," said Victor hastily as he pushed Declan in and closed the door. Declan recognized the man as the person who was waiting at the door for Victor earlier this morning.

"So you're the boy with the powers of demons?" asked Collin with excitement in his eyes.

"Wow, you don't really waste any time on small talk, do you?" Declan was startled by the first comment made to him by Collin.

"Sorry, for my bluntness, but it's just so fascinating. I've read about people like you, but I've never really met one until now," replied Collin who looked at Declan as if he was looking at an interesting animal at the zoo.

"People like me? You mean, you know why I can do the things that I do?" asked Declan as his eyes widened. *Finally, maybe I can make sense of all of this.* He felt his hands start trembling with excitement.

"Before, I reveal too much, prove to me what you can do," demanded Collin as he sat back as if a movie was about to start.

"Brother, I'm sorry, but we do not have time for this right now. This house has been compromised and we must move," pleaded Victor throwing up his arms.

"Yes, you are right, Brother. Have you secured the vials for transport? And is our little rehab patient ready to go?" asked Collins now in a serious tone.

"Yes, they are in the carrier bag on the dining table. Kyle is upstairs. He can go at any time," replied Victor as if giving a status report.

"So, are you like Victor's boss or something? You're kind of young for such a position," asked Declan trying to figure out what was going on.

"Declan, why are you here?" asked Victor sounding irritated.

"Oh, that's right. I am here to tell you that the FBI is after you. They think you're some kind of serial killer. Which I've got to say, I'm not too surprised. When you kidnapped me last night, I was thinking that same thing myself. Maybe you have that serial killer look. I mean, you do come off quite odd being a buff old dude and all," said Declan with a smirk on his face. *Wow, I've been spending way too much time with Keira and Caleb. Their incessant need to sass each other has rubbed off on me.*

"So what else is new? Those two FBI agents have been after me for the past few years. How did you know about them?" asked Victor as he picked up a travel bag and started stuffing his belongings into it.

༺༻

"Deck's been in there for quite a while now. You don't think that something's happened, do you? His co-worker looks kind of strange," asked Keira concerned as she recalled the obscenely muscular old man who greeted Declan at the door earlier.

"He said that he needed to pick something up from that weird looking buff old guy; maybe he's so old he's forgotten where he put it," replied Caleb nonchalantly as he continued to play a game on his phone.

"Hey, is that Tristan walking up the driveway?" asked Keira confused.

Caleb snapped up when Keira said that and said, "That is Tristan. I wonder if Zoe's back from New York."

"Is that all you care about? What about why Tristan might know Deck's co-worker? Or why he and his sister suddenly disappeared?" asked Keira with a minor sound of irritation with Caleb's one-track mind.

"He doesn't seem to have seen us. We should go greet him and see how Zoe's doing," said Caleb completely ignoring his sister's concerns. He was about to open his car door when Tristan kick down the front door.

"Whoa, what that heck is he doing?" said Caleb, shocked by what he saw. It took him several seconds to recover from his shock, but Keira had already dashed out of the car and started to run toward the house.

"Wait, Keira!" he called to his sister, but she continued at full speed. "You are always so impulsive! You ... tomboy!" he muttered under his breath.

∞⨀∞

"Alright, give me back the Sullivans and nobody gets hurt!" yelled Tristan as he stepped through the broken door. Victor and Collin stared blankly at the teenager who had just busted through the front door.

"You! I knew there was something strange about you! So you're in on this! An ordinary bunch of humans, my ass!" yelled Tristan as he noticed Declan.

"What? In on what? I think you've misunderstood. What are you doing here anyway?" asked Declan confused about the whole situation.

As Tristan focused on Declan, Victor reached into his pocket and produced his flask of Holy water and crucifix. He opened the flask and flung holy water toward Tristan. At the same time, he held his crucifix in front of him and shouted, "Demon, how dare you make demands against the servants of the Lord Almighty!"

Tristan moved with a blur. Not knowing what was being flung at him, he dodged the holy water. He zoomed up to Victor and pushed him so hard that he flew back ten feet into the kitchen. Before he could continue to pursue Victor, Declan jumped on top of him trying to restrain him on the ground.

"Oh, so you want to dance little exorcist …?" said Tristan as he started to whirl.

Keira had just entered the house when she saw Tristan and Declan become a blur in the middle of the living room. Her eyes widened as it reminded her of the events of the previous night.

"What are you talking about, Tristan? I am not an exorcist," yelled Declan as he held on tight. He was being spun so fast that the entire room looked like a streak of colors.

"Then what are you? Why did you help them capture my parents?" asked Tristan with rage in his voice.

"What are you talking about? I'm not sure what I am. What are you? You seem to be able to do the same things I can do," asked Declan still holding on. This made Tristan stop as he was baffled by it all.

All the while, Collin slung something that looked like a whip across the room and as it connected to Tristan's legs, it wrapped itself around several times. Tristan looked down, something that looked like a chain made with crucifixes had wound itself around his ankles.

"Got you now, demon!" declared Collin as he rushed over and flung holy water all over Tristan and Declan.

"I'm not a low-life demon, you half-wit!" yelled Tristan as he broke the chain that was wound around his ankle and grabbed Collin by the neck with his hand.

Collin made choking sounds as Tristan lifted him off the ground.

"Stop!" yelled Declan as he tried to pull Tristan's arm back down to lower Collin back to the ground. Keira and Caleb, who had just entered the house, watched with shock. With his last bit of strength before he blacked out, Collin pulled out a Taser from his pocket and shot it at Tristan. All three of them collapsed on the floor.

CHAPTER 25
-DECLAN-

"Deck? Deck? He's coming to," said Keira as she hovered over Declan.

"What … what's going on?" asked Declan as his vision slowly came back, and he saw Keira directly above him. His cheeks immediately blushed but since his cheeks were already red due to the shock of electricity that he had just endured, nobody noticed.

"Oh, thank goodness you're okay, Deck. Praise Jesus!" exclaimed Keira as she gave him a big hug.

Declan looked over on his right, and he saw Tristan still unconscious. The events of the morning came rushing back to him, and he shrieked back from Tristan.

"It's okay, dude. We tied him up good with steel chains. He won't be going Superman on us, but you have a lot of explaining to do," declared Caleb with his arms crossed.

Declan sat up. Victor handed him a bottle of water. "Being tasered twice within a 24-hour period has got to take a toll on you."

"We're still waiting for that explanation," said Keira, matching Caleb's posture with her arms crossed.

"Guys, I don't really know what's going on or how come I could do those things," replied Declan not wanting to review the secrets of Victor and Collin.

"Maybe I can explain some of that," answered Collin. "I promised that I'd tell you what I knew once you've proved some of your abilities to me, and let me say between the two of you," he gestured to Declan and Tristan, "I've seen my share."

Collin sat down and took in a big sip of his tea. "From what I've read in the journals of our Brothers from long ago, you are what we called a P-born or Possessed Born."

"What?" Declan jumped. "You mean I am possessed after all?" Goose bumps spread across his body as his heart pounded in anticipation to Collin's answer.

"No, and don't cut in again. Got it, kid?" Collin said as he glared up from his cup.

Declan shrieked back at Collin's sudden demeanor change. *That does seem more in line with his GI look.* Suddenly, he thought he saw some movement, so he turned toward Tristan, but saw that he was still unconscious.

Dropping back into his excited scholar demeanor, Collin continued. "I'm sure that Victor has already filled you in on the existence of demons and their origins. Something very strange happens when a pregnant woman gets possessed. As the baby is developing within the womb of a possessed individual, it tends to develop some of the demonic powers that the possessed individual has. Of course, these women rarely survive long enough to give birth, but when they do, these children are considered to be born of the possessed, which later became Possessed Born, and finally P-born. I thought that the demons had forbidden the possession of pregnant women, but now I've actually met two in person. I can't tell you how exciting this is."

Collin looked as if he was about to jump up and down with glee while the Millers had an awkward look of disbelief on their face.

"Wait, why was it forbidden?" asked Declan as his eyes widened with interest. Collin raised an eyebrow, and Declan's excitement diminished.

"Well, we've been fighting against the demons since the Flood. Whenever we've encountered a possessed individual, we would exorcise the demon and trap it in some sort of container. We would then move these trapped demons from one place to another constantly to prevent the demons from finding their location and freeing their brethren. We got to a point where we understood the weaknesses of the demons so well that we found a way to keep demons away even if they found the location of the containers at one time or another. Well … for a while anyway. So they started purposely creating P-borns in the hopes of creating an army that we seemed powerless against. Praise be to God that the P-borns decided to side with humanity and helped us hunt down more demons than ever before. Because of this betrayal, the demons vowed to never create anymore P-borns and the possession of pregnant women was forbidden ever since."

"That has got to be the most ludicrous story I've ever heard," said Caleb with the most cynical tone Declan had ever heard him use. And Declan had seen Caleb's cynical side every time Keira or his parents brought up the topic of religion.

Once again, Collin dropped into his GI demeanor, "What did you just say, son! You calling me a liar?"

"No! But how can this all be possible? Wouldn't we have at least heard about something like this before?"

"Where do you think stories about the Greek heroes who had the might of the gods came from? These heroes would always side with humanity and fight with the so-called gods that oppressed the people. Those were all historical events, though maybe exaggerated, between the P-borns and the demons that had posed as gods during the ancient times. As a matter of fact, in every culture, you will find myths about humans who had some sort of special abilities and fought against some of the evil gods of their culture. These aren't mere coincidences," Victor jumped in before things between Caleb and Collin escalated.

"So you knew all along?" asked Declan with a sense of betrayal. "My mother's insanity, it must have been due to demonic possession."

"No, I had my suspicions, but I couldn't be sure. However, after witnessing the fight between the two of you, it was apparent to me that you two were the same. Since I had recently exorcised the Sullivan seniors, it was a no-brainer that Tristan must have been a P-born and by extension you must also be a P-born. Now as to your mother's condition, I'm unsure about that. But enough with the history lesson; we really got to get out of here. This location isn't safe," replied Victor with true worry in his eyes that Declan hadn't seen before, despite the demon encounters over the past 24-hours.

"Alright Brother, you have the address to the new safe house. I will take the vials and our rehab patient to the next transport location," answered Collins as he picked up the carrier bag with the vials.

As they were still talking, an unmarked white van pulled up to the driveway. Out of the van came a tall man wearing a white suit and about half a dozen men in black suits. The tall man had dark curly hair and green eyes. He walked with an aura of confidence as he approached the broken doorway.

"Shit, they've found us. It's Luca Davis," said Collin sounding nervous.

"Oh, if it isn't Collin Weiss and Victor Roesch. How lovely it is to see you two again. My, how you've aged. You were just a teenager when we last met Collin, and Victor, time has especially been harsh on you," said Luca with a smug smile on his face as he walked up to the broken down front door.

"I see that your taste in clothing is as poor as ever, Luca. Now leave before I trap you in a punching back and use you for my training," said Victor with steel in his voice.

"Your idle threats are worthless. Now, hand over the vials and I will promise you a quick death," said Luca as he looked at his hand and started picking at his nails.

Collin dangled the carrier bag in front of him and said, "Why don't you come in and get it?"

Luca took a step forward but appeared to have hit an invisible wall. His face had an expression of irritation, but only for a few seconds. "Must we do this every time? Your blessings are worthless when I've got goons," said Luca sounding bored. He yelled to the men in black suits, "Go and retrieve the bag!"

The goons started walking toward the front door when Tristan, who had pretended to be unconscious, broke out of the steel chains, grabbed the carrier bag, and jumped so high that he broke through the second story of the house. He then crashed through a window and escaped out the back.

Luca seemed taken aback, but quickly recovered. "Kill them all," he commanded and pursued Tristan.

The goons pulled out guns and pointed them at the five in the house. Declan moved in a blur and knocked the first goon so hard that he flew out of the house and across the street. Seeing how quickly Declan moved, three of the other goons swiftly turned their guns toward Declan, but Caleb, Collin, and Victor jumped on top of them before they could fire. Declan blurred again and kicked the other two goons, sending them flying against the sides of the living room. And finally, grabbing a lamp, Declan knocked out the three goons who were being restrained. Declan sat down as he hyperventilated. He was not used to using his abilities for such a prolonged period of time, and as Victor had said earlier, being tasered twice really had taken its toll on him.

"So ... what now? Do we go after them?" asked Caleb still slightly shocked at what his best friend whom he'd known for a decade now could do.

"We wouldn't even know where to go," said Keira as she stared at the hole that Tristan had made in the ceiling.

"Luca is one of the most powerful channelers I have ever encountered. I don't think that it will be long before he catches up to Tristan and takes the vials from him," said Victor in a defeated tone.

"So ... what do we do? Just sit here and sulk?" asked Declan as his shoulders slumped.

"Knowing Luca, he wouldn't hold onto the vials too long, he's going to want to destroy them as soon as he can. Based on the data I've gathered about the area, the only foundry near here doesn't have the capability of melting Tungsten, so … that leaves Jacksonville," said Collin as he squinted his eyes, deep in thought.

"Wait a minute!" Declan thought back to the conversation with his uncle a couple days ago. "My uncle told me that the foundry that he works at in Oakland was putting in a new furnace that can help them cast super alloys. Would that be enough to melt Tungsten?"

"Shit! We have to get there right now! If they release those demons from the vials, I don't even want to think about what they'd do," declared Collin with urgency.

"Let's go!" declared Keira excited about the chase.

"Keira, we just found out that there are demons in this world, and you want to go and chase them down?" asked Caleb unsure of what to think.

"We've been taught that demons exist our entire lives Caleb; it's in the Bible. If only you weren't such a slacker in Sunday school …" mocked Keira.

"Fine, even if I can accept that fact, why do we want to get mixed up in all of this?" asked Caleb wide-eyed at his sister's response.

"Because Deck is already involved, and I'm going to stand by him no matter what! Where are you going to stand?" asked Keira with steel in her eyes.

"No guys! It's too dangerous! I want you guys to stay behind!" pleaded Declan.

"I'm not afraid. I have the Spirit of the Living God within me. Of whom shall I fear; of whom shall I be afraid?" Keira said boldly reciting scripture as Caleb started shaking his head.

"Here we go again, Prayer Warrior Princess Keira, not afraid of anything because God is with her. Keira, this is not just like praying. You saw the goons that dude had right? They all had guns. No amount of praying will protect you from that!" said Caleb as he stared intently into his sister's eyes.

"Guys, there is no time to argue here, either come with us or don't, but we have to get going!" demanded Victor as he rushed toward his car with Collin.

"Sorry, guys, but you're not going," said Declan as he moved in a blur toward Caleb's car and punctured one of the tires. "I can get there faster. I'll meet you there!" he said to Victor as he disappeared in a blur.

"Deck!" screamed Keira as Declan disappeared.

CHAPTER 26
-DECLAN-

Declan arrived at the entrance of the SCG Foundry in Oakland and he saw that the entrance had been forced opened.

We were correct about them.

He could hear sounds clanging inside the foundry, and he rushed in. As his eyes adjusted to the dim lighting inside, he saw Tristan facing off Luca. Tristan looked ragged and beaten up while Luca's white suit looked pristine.

"Give the vials back!" demanded Tristan with rage in his voice.

"Take them from me, young demon," said Luca daring Tristan to strike again.

Tristan blurred into motion, but it was as if Luca anticipated every move and either blocked or dodged out of the way half a second quicker.

"You should stand down while you still can, young demon. Identify yourself. Who do you work under?" demanded Luca.

"I don't work under anyone, you filthy demon! And stop calling me young demon!" yelled Tristan as he hyperventilated.

"A rogue? I can see why you couldn't tell that my demon clearly out ranks you. Stand down and I might forget the whole ordeal," said Luca in a bored tone.

"There is no rank; I am not a demon," shouted Tristan in frustration, and he rushed once again at Luca.

As Luca easily dodged the attacks from Tristan, Declan rushed at him from the back. He was sure that he would get his strike in, but Luca turned just in time and caught his fist before it connected.

"Another young demon that needs to learn his place!" Luca said as he grabbed the rest of Declan's arm and swung him toward a stack of sand molds. Declan crashed against the molds and they shattered. Then, as Tristan tried to sweep Luca's feet from underneath him, Luca caught Tristan by the hair and banged his head against the side of the furnace.

Tristan recovered and jumped back away from Luca only to find Declan standing beside him. "All right, it seems that we have a common enemy right now. Let's work together to beat him first and we fight for the vials afterward?" asked Declan as he kept a close eye on Luca.

"Deal!" said Tristan and both of them rushed at Luca at the same time.

"Insolent little demons!" shouted Luca as he ducked under both their attacks and swept at their feet.

The two jumped upward and came down with a drop kick shouting, "We're not demons!"

The fight continued for another couple of minutes as the two worked together against Luca, but to no avail. They were not able to get a single hit in, and both of them were getting worn out.

"Alright, I've had enough of these kiddy games. Let me show you the difference between a channeler and a possessed," said Luca as his right fist started to glow brightly. He opened his hand and shot out a bolt of lightning toward the two. The two jumped backward but were blasted back by the debris that was torn from the earth when the bolt hit the ground where they were previously standing.

"There is no way that the likes of you will be able to defeat me!" demanded Luca as he started to charge another lightning bolt in his fist.

"Who said, I was trying to defeat you?" asked Declan with a grin on his face. "I was merely stalling for reinforcements."

Luca's instincts took over, and he jumped backward ten feet just before a splash of water hit where he was previously standing. Luca's eyes trailed to the source of the water and found Collin holding a pressure washer nozzle while Victor hovered over the pressure washer. Collin followed Luca with the nozzle, and the water chased him as he blurred throughout the foundry blasting sand molds, wooden patterns, and furnaces.

"Oh, you better run, you piece of shit!" yelled Collin with a maniacal laughter.

Tristan took the distraction that the two exorcists gave Luca, and he vanished into thin air. He reappeared directly behind Luca, grabbing the carrier bag from him. Luca retaliated by releasing a bolt of lightning from his hand, hitting Tristan in the back. Clothing and flesh exploded from Tristan's back as he flew across the foundry. Luca followed Tristan to where he landed and retrieved the carrier bag.

The sound of a bell came from the furnace indicating that it had reached the intended temperature. Luca rushed toward the furnace and threw the entire carrier bag into it. Collin, who had anticipated his move, blasted him with water. Luca writhed on the ground in agony.

"How did you do that?" asked Declan surprised at what took Luca down.

"Instant holy water blaster," said Collin as he directed Declan's attention to Victor who was constantly blessing the water as it entered the pressure washer.

Declan then rushed to Tristan's side to check on him as Collin kept the blast of water on Luca. Tristan was bleeding out fast and his breathing was slowing down.

"We have to get him help!" demanded Declan as he tried to pick Tristan up.

Before Declan could pick Tristan up, he noticed six dark writhing shapes coming out of the furnace.

"The demons! They're released!" shouted Declan as horror filled his expression.

The shades swarmed outward and tried to exit the foundry through the door and windows, but appeared to have hit a wall.

"They're not going anywhere. We've already blessed all the possible exit points before hand," said Collin as Victor started to pray and lifted up an uncapped vial.

Luca rolled himself out of the blast of water once the flow of water was no longer holy. Just as he moved away from the water, one of the doors of the side entrance opened, and Caleb and Keira rushed in. Luca blurred far away from the blast of water and sent a bolt of lightning toward Declan.

Declan spun through the air as the bolt of lightning hit him in the arm. Pain exploded inside of him as his flesh burned off his arm. He breathed heavily to push the pain out of his mind as he hit the floor and clutched at his arm.

Seeing Declan on the floor and bleeding, Keira rushed toward Declan. As Keira moved, one of the dark entities noticed her and rushed toward her. Declan watched in horror and wanted to scream out to her but was still incapacitated by the pain. As the demon approached Keira, Declan noticed a light that seemed to radiate from her body, and the demon had to shield its eyes. It then redirected itself and headed for Caleb. The demon entered him, and he stood completely stiff. Terror welled up in his eyes, and the veins on his neck started to show.

Caleb collapsed to the floor clutching himself, and he writhed in agony. Luca rushed toward Caleb, swooped him up, and crashed through the wall of the building using Caleb's body. Through the opening that Luca created, the other shades also escaped.

"Caleb!" screamed Keira as she ran toward the opening in the wall and watched Luca disappear in the distance with her brother.

Declan tried to get up and pursue Luca, but as he stood, his knees became weak, and he fell back to the ground.

"Deck!" shouted Keira as she rushed back to him.

"Caleb! I must save him!" Declan cried in a weak voice as more blood flowed from his arm and all went black.

CHAPTER 27
-DECLAN-

Declan opened his eyes and realized that he was in his bed. He turned to the right to take a look at his clock on his nightstand and saw that Caleb was sitting by his bed.

"Caleb! You're okay! Thank goodness!" cried Declan as a tear rolled out from the corner of his eye.

"Deck, are you okay now?" asked Caleb in a sad tone. "I mean, are you … you again?"

"What are you talking about? Of course, I'm me! Are you … you?" asked Declan remembering the image of the demon entering Caleb's body.

Roy walked into the room with a sad expression on his face and said, "Oh, Deck, you're awake."

"Yeah, Uncle, what's going on?" asked Declan as he tried to sit up, only to notice that there were restraints around his wrists and ankles. Declan struggled against the restraints and shouted, "What is all of this? Why am I restrained?"

"Son, calm down. I don't blame you. This wasn't your fault …" said Roy as tears rolled out of his eyes.

"What happened? What isn't my fault? What's going on?" asked Declan confused by everyone's mood.

"Your Aunt Jenny, Deck ..." replied Roy as he choked up and couldn't finish.

"What happened to Auntie?" demanded Declan, now scared.

"You drowned her, Deck!" said Caleb as tears rolled out of his eyes.

Shocked by what Caleb said, Declan took a look at his surroundings once again and realized that he was not in his bedroom but in one of the patient rooms on the fifth floor of his workplace.

ഔരൽ

"No!" screamed Declan as he sat up in a bed he didn't recognize, sweat dripping from his face.

Keira came rushing in through the door of the bedroom. "Deck, you're awake!"

"Aunt Jenny! I killed her ..." sobbed Declan as Keira came to his side and held him.

"What? It was just a nightmare, Deck. Your Aunt Jenny is fine; I just spoke with her an hour ago," said Keira as she stroked Declan's back as the muscles on his back relaxed.

After a few seconds, Declan realized that he was holding Keira so close to his body and his heart raced even more than it had before. Keira backed away from Declan a little so that she could cup her hands on Declan's face and look into his eyes.

"What ... what happened? Where are we?" asked Declan as he looked around them. He seemed to be in an unfamiliar bedroom.

"We're in another safe house that the exorcists have set up here. You tried to chase after Luca and Caleb, but you passed out due to blood loss. You've been sleeping for almost ten hours now," explained Keira with concern in her eyes.

"And Caleb? Where is he now?" asked Declan almost desperate.

"I don't know," said Keira as tears welled up in her eyes.

"I'll find him Keira! And I'll bring him back! I swear to you!"

"Oh Deck, thank you, but I'm coming with you. We'll bring him back together," demanded Keira as her eyes hardened.

"No, Keira, it's too dangerous. I don't know what I'd do if something were to happen to you, too," pleaded Declan.

"Deck, I have to do this! He's my brother!" said Keira. Declan gazed into her eyes and knew that there was no convincing her otherwise.

"Fine, we'll go get him back together," Declan relented.

"Let me change your bandages first. We'll go once you're well," replied Keira as she went to get some fresh bandages.

Keira came back with a bottle of peroxide, bandages, and some cotton balls. She carefully unwrapped the bloody bandages from Declan's arm. Taking a cotton ball, she dipped it in the peroxide and started to dab at the dried blood on Declan's arm. Keira's eyes widened, "Your wound, it's gone!" said Keira with amazement in her voice.

"What?" asked Declan as he looked down to examine his arm. He moved his arm around in circles and said, "It's true! I don't feel any pain at all."

"So ... what? Another P-born thing?" said Keira incredulously.

"I guess ..." replied Declan still shocked at the appearance of his arm.

"Oh, by the way, I believe that you were missing this," said Keira as she held out a necklace that had Declan's mother's pendant dangling at the end of it.

Declan sat up and grasped for it. He held it so tight as if he thought that it would run away if he let go. As he held it, a feeling of hope started to build inside of him. He felt that maybe everything might work out after all.

"Yes! How did you ...? Where did you ...?" asked Declan so excited he couldn't complete the thought.

"I think you dropped it during the fight with Nelly the other night. After you left with the EMTs, Caleb and I found it. I meant to give it to you that night when we waited for you at home, but you rushed us out so quickly, it totally slipped my mind," said Keira as she almost choked up again at the mention of Caleb.

Declan looked down at the pendant, now in his hand. "This pendant … I found it after my mother had been taken away, but for some reason, it doesn't remind me of who my mother is now, but who she was … before. I don't know why, but this pendant makes me feel whole. I've felt so lost since I misplaced it. Thank you so much, Keira," Declan said as he felt warm tears filling his eyes.

ಬುಃಲ

Tristan woke up coughing as coagulated blood came out of his mouth.

"Trist! Are you okay?" asked Zoe as she knelt down by her brother.

Tristan couldn't answer as he continued to cough.

Zoe patted his back as the coughing continued. "I think you'll be fine once you get all the blood out of your lungs. Your wound site appears to have healed."

"Zoe … how did I get here?" asked Tristan as he looked around at his surroundings.

"Caleb called me and told me that you had stolen some vials and they were tracking you to a foundry in Oakland. When I got there, I saw a demon bust out of the building. When I entered the foundry, I found you were injured, so I took you back to the hotel. What happened?" asked Zoe.

"I tracked down the exorcist who had captured Mom and Dad. I had retrieved them when a demon … well, a channeler … attacked me and took them from me," replied Tristan trying not to say too much so as to not trigger another coughing fit.

Zoe placed her hand on Tristan's and said, "Trist, please … just give up this search for Mom and Dad. I've already lost them, and I don't want to lose you, too. I don't care if we never find out about what we are and who Mom and Dad were. Can't we just live the rest of our lives out as normal people?" asked Zoe as she looked into his eyes.

"Zoe, I know what we are," he said, and he explained to her what he had overheard when he was pretending to be unconscious at the exorcist's house.

"So ... our mother was possessed when she was pregnant with us and that's why we are the way we are?" asked Zoe with sadness in her eyes.

"I guess, but how does Dad come into all of this? And why did they stay in those bodies" wondered Tristan.

"Could it be that they possessed them first, got married, and then had us?" asked Zoe hopefully.

"That's not the way demons work from my experience," replied Tristan with a cynical tone.

"I guess we'll never know," said Zoe, still sad.

"We can still try to find out," suggested Tristan as he looked around the room.

"No," said Zoe sadly, "I'd rather not find out. I don't want to know, Trist! Can you just let me preserve my memory of them?"

The doorbell of the penthouse sounded, and Zoe walked towards the door. "Oh, I figured you might want to eat once you were awake and ordered room service."

Zoe exited Tristan's room to get the door. Tristan got out of his bed and walked over to his jacket. He reached into his pocket and carefully pulled out two capped metallic vials using a handkerchief, making sure there was no direct contact with his fingers.

I'll get all the answers I want now that I have you.

ಬಿಡ

"So, I heard that you guys are planning on searching for Caleb," said Victor as Declan and Keira were walking down the staircase of the new safe house.

"It's my fault that he's been captured," replied Declan, "I have to get him back."

"Come. Sit," Victor gestured toward the couches in the living room.

Declan looked around. The new safe house looked exactly the same as the old safe house.

Geez, talk about being creatures of habit. Declan sat.

"Look, Victor, there's no point in trying to stop us. We've made up our minds." Keira sat down next to Declan.

"Who said I was planning on stopping you? I'm merely offering my help."

Both Declan and Keira's eyes widened. They were both determined on finding Caleb, but in reality, they both didn't know where to even start looking. Their hearts eased up a little as the words came out of Victor's mouth.

"How are you going to help us?" asked Declan as a smile crept up his face.

"Join my organization, and I promise to use all our resources to locate Caleb and help you retrieve him," he replied confidently.

"Wait, if this is some sort of sales pitch to force me to join your 'club,' you can forget about it," said Declan as anger flared up in him. *Once again, someone is trying to force Christianity on me!*

"How do you plan on fighting Luca and the possibility of other channelers when you do find where they are keeping Caleb?" asked Victor as he crossed his arms.

"With my fists!" Declan spat as he held his fists up.

"Yes, and we saw how well that fared against Luca yesterday," replied Victor flatly.

"I'll join," declared Keira stone-faced as Declan turned to stare at her.

"Keira, don't let him strong-arm you into joining."

"No, I'm not being strong-armed. I refuse to be defenseless against these creatures. I want to learn to fight them," said Keira as her jaw clenched. Declan stared blankly at her and images of the blinding light that emanated from her as the shade tried to enter her replayed in his mind.

Resigned, Declan said, "Fine, I'll bite. What do we have to do? Wait … do I need to become Catholic?"

Confused by the sudden question, "Why would you ask that?" asked Victor.

"Well, all the holy water and the rosary … I had just assumed that you were all Catholics. I mean, I don't know too much about all those denominations and stuff," replied Declan in an unsure manner.

"Declan, we exorcists don't really care too much for denominations. We're all the same body of Christ. And of course, with a body, there have to be different body parts. But every part must work together for a body to function. Do you understand that?" asked Victor.

Declan tried to continue the discussion, but Keira stopped him, "Deck, can you just relax, no one's forcing you to convert to anything."

"Well … to be an effective exorcist, one must have faith," replied Victor as he stared deep into Declan's eyes. But then he noticed the pendant around his neck. "What is that you have around your neck, Declan?"

Immediately, Declan's hand shot up to his pendant and clutched it as if someone was trying to take it from him. "What this? It's my mother's pendant. I've been wearing it since I was seven," replied Declan defensively.

"I did not see you with it the other day when I brought you to the other safe house," Victor said suspiciously.

"You mean, when you kidnapped me?" Declan responded indignantly. He continued, "I dropped it during my fight with Nelly, and Keira just returned it to me. Why are you making it such a big deal?"

"I've seen such pendants before," said Victor in a serious tone, "the hunters wear similar pendants."

"What? So what are you insinuating?" asked Declan now standing up with hands balling into fists, but then he remembered his conversation with Victor the other morning, *"The method of choice for a hunter would be drowning. I find it ... strange ... that your mother, in her state of dementia, would stumble upon feasible methods of dealing with demonic possession,"* Victor had said.

Declan sat back down in an instant of realization, "My mother was a hunter?"

"That would seem to be the case," said Victor, now sounding very sure of himself.

"What are hunters?" asked Keira seemingly lost with the whole conversation.

"They hunt demons ... but end up killing the hosts," answered Declan now in a deflated tone.

"Well, they hunt many things, but yes they all boil down to demons," Victor responded.

"What? There are other things too? Like what? Vampires?" asked Kiera.

"Yes, vampires are real. But not as ridiculously romanticized as we see in the movies today. They are enthralled men who have sworn loyalty to Gaap, a very powerful demon, and help him gather power by absorbing life force through human blood," replied Victor with a smirk.

"You have got to be joking me," said Keira.

"Absorbing life force? What about succubusses ... wait succubi? What is the plural form of succubus? Whatever ... Don't they do the same thing," asked Declan with a grin on his face.

"If you're referring to demons who sex men to death to suck out their life force, that's just men's wishful thinking," replied Victor with an eyebrow raised.

Keira punched Declan in the arm and said, "Pig!"

"Wait, what about witches, fairies, and—"

"So many questions! Am I going to regret asking you to join?" asked Victor. He threw his hands up at a loss while Declan and Keira grinned at him.

ⴲⵣⴳ

"Deck, make sure you pack your warm jacket," reminded Jenny as Declan was packing his luggage.

"So … what job is this again that you have to travel to Atlanta for training? And why do you have to go so soon?" asked Roy as he walked into Declan's room and placed an arm around Jenny.

"It's a job that my co-worker introduced me to. It's a … freelance traveling UAP gig. It pays a lot more, and I get to travel. You said that you want me to journey out and get out of my comfort zone, so here I go," replied Declan as he continued to pack.

"Yeah, I had mentioned that, but I meant going to college. If you'd only given me some more time. Once the foundry is completed after all the repairs needed because of the random vandalism last week, I'll be able to work more hours, and we can send you to college then. You don't have to worry so much about the money." Roy placed his other hand on Declan's shoulder.

"Uncle, please, I told you, it wasn't just to bring back more money. It's just something I wanted to try out, okay?" replied Declan, hating himself for having to lie to his uncle and aunt.

Jenny squeezed Roy's hand tightly signaling him to stop and said, "Deck, please just take good care of yourself, and give us a call daily so that we know that you are doing alright."

"I'll try Auntie. I don't know how demanding the training is going to be, but every chance I get, I'll call," Declan promised.

ⴲⵣⴳ

Declan drove up to the Millers' house and as he saw the front door open he wished that Caleb would walk through it. However, Keira walked out alone with her suitcase. Declan got out of the car and helped her put it into the trunk.

"So, what did you tell your parents about where you were going and where Caleb was?" asked Declan sadly.

"I haven't yet. They won't be back from that leadership conference until this afternoon. I left them a note," replied Keira in the same sad tone.

"Saying ...?" nudged Declan curiously.

"Telling them the exact reason why Caleb and I were not there," replied Keira as if confused by why Declan would even ask.

"Really? You wrote that demons captured Caleb and that you were going to join a league of exorcists to get him back?" replied Declan sarcastically.

"Yes, maybe not quite so bluntly, but yes. That's the truth," said Keira rolling her eyes.

Declan's jaw dropped. "How do you think your parents will take that?" asked Declan concerned.

"I don't know, and that's why I decided to leave a note," replied Keira not looking at him.

"So ... you are afraid of some things after all," jibed Declan with a smile on his face.

"Hey, I'll take avoidance over lying any day," replied Keira with a small punch to Declan's arm. "So, it's gonna be a seven-hour drive up to Atlanta, right?" asked Keira as she stretched.

His heart pounded when he realized that he was going to be alone in the car with Keira for the next couple hours. "Hey, Keira ... listen ... I've been meaning to talk to you about us —"

"Oh Declan, you have no idea how long I had waited to have this conversation with you ... but ... I made a promise to God that I will not think about anything else until I get Caleb back! You see ... it's all my fault! He didn't want to go to the foundry that day. I forced him to take me. I need to take responsibility for it." Hot tears streamed down Keira's face.

"Keira, if anyone is at fault, it's me. I was the one to asked you guys to drive me to the safe house in the first place. I promise you, that I will get Caleb back for you even if it's the last thing I do."

Keira didn't answer but just continued to sob.

"I want to stop by the behavioral center and chat with my mom before we go," said Declan.

EPILOGUE

Declan squeezed Keira's hand as he walked down the hall of the fifth floor of the behavioral center while at the same time clutching the pendant around his neck. His heart pounded as he placed his hand on the doorknob to his mother's room. Keira placed her other hand on top of his as he turned the knob.

His mom was restrained on the bed as they walked into the room.

"Mom?" said Declan nervously as he approached.

Her eyes opened as she heard his voice. Her eyes were filled with menace and hatred as she struggled against her restraints.

"Demon child! I will kill you!" she screamed as she continued to pull on her restrains. Her veins bulged as she strained.

Declan's heart broke as he watched his mother struggle.

Talking over her screams, tears rolled down his face. "Mom, I'm going away for a while. I'll be back when we find Caleb. I love you."

Keira covered her eyes in horror as tears came down her face. Declan grabbed her by the arm and led her back to the door, but stopped before he opened it.

Do I dare try? No, it just can't be, he thought.

"I'll … meet you outside," said Declan as he turned back toward his mother.

Keira nodded and walked outside.

Declan's heart pounded so hard he felt as if his heart would jump out of his chest. He walked up to his mother, took out a crucifix from his pocket, and pressed it down onto his mother's arm.

ABOUT THE AUTHOR

A project manager by profession but a modern renaissance man by nature, Michael Pang has dabbled in many different areas in his career. From working with steam turbines to eventually switching into the world of IT, his plethora of experience highlights his personality - he's a person always searching for more knowledge.

Michael was born in Hong Kong in 1983. His family immigrated to San Francisco when he was three and eventually landed in Florida. After graduating from high school, Michael gained his degree in mechanical engineering from Georgia Tech. Despite his currently demanding work schedule, Michael is very involved in activities at his local Project Management Institute Chapter where he fulfills his passion for teaching as the Vice President of Education. But, his desire to serve and help others doesn't end there, he's an avid Christian and very active in his local church. He loves kids and has two daughters of his own with his lovely wife and volunteers at children's church in his ministry.

He speaks fluent Cantonese and Mandarin and in his free time enjoys reading, writing, eating, cooking, playing music, dancing, singing, and watching musicals. One of his mottos is "Every day that he hasn't learned something new is a day wasted."

Get the latest news on the book series by going to my website...

http://www.InTheEyesOfMadness.com

www.ingramcontent.com/pod-product-compliance
Lightning Source LLC
Chambersburg PA
CBHW020628110726
47899CB00002B/695